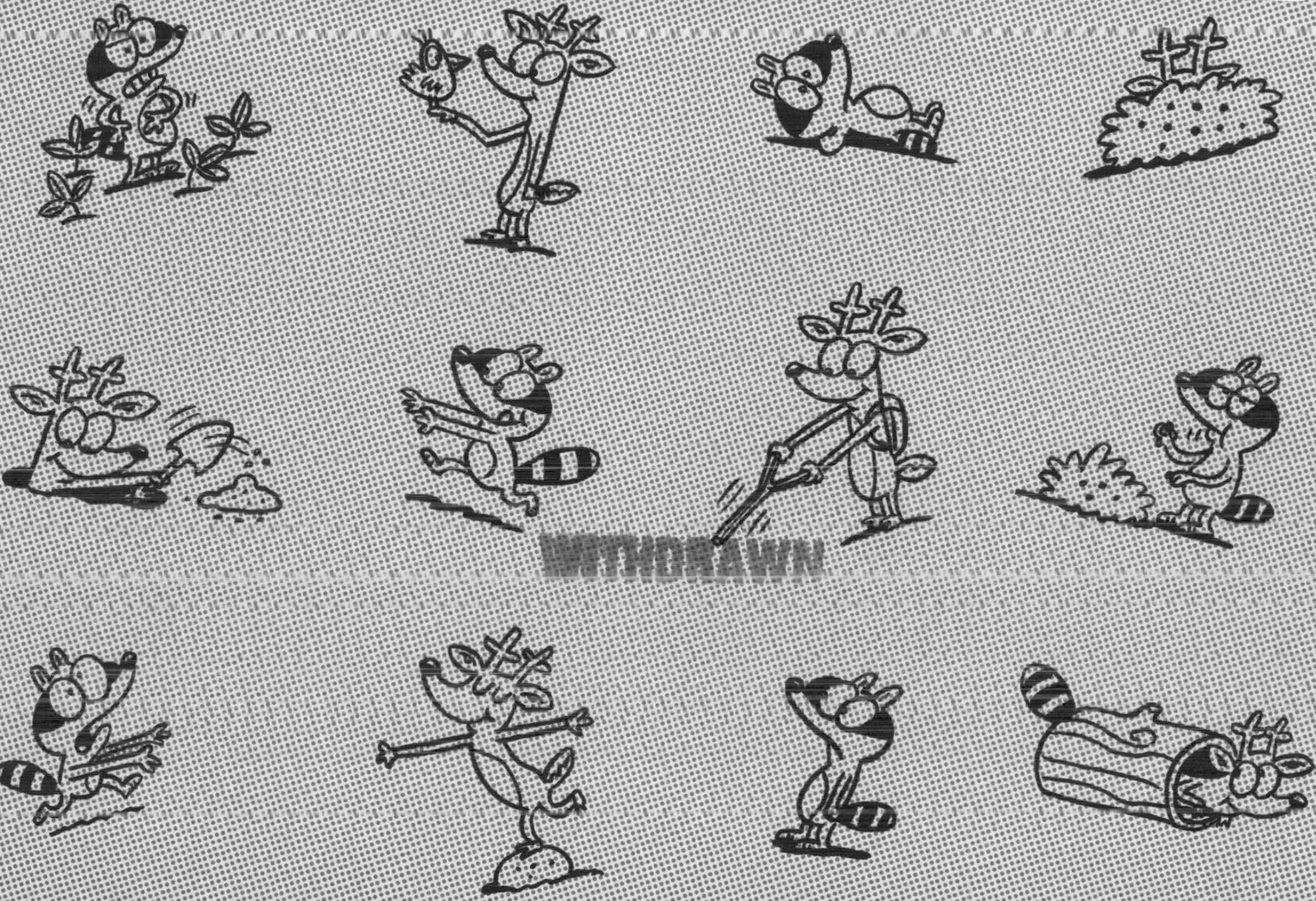

Copyright ©2010 Ethan Long

Balloon Toons™ is a registered
trademark of Harriet Ziefert, Inc.

All rights reserved/CIP data is available.

Published in the United States 2010 by
Blue Apple Books
515 Valley Street, Maplewood, NJ 07040
www.blueapplebooks.com

Distributed in the U.S. by Chronicle Books
First Edition
Printed in China 09/10
ISBN: 978-1-60905-034-4

2 4 6 8 10 9 7 5 3 1

BALLOON TOONS

Ethan Long

Rick & Rack

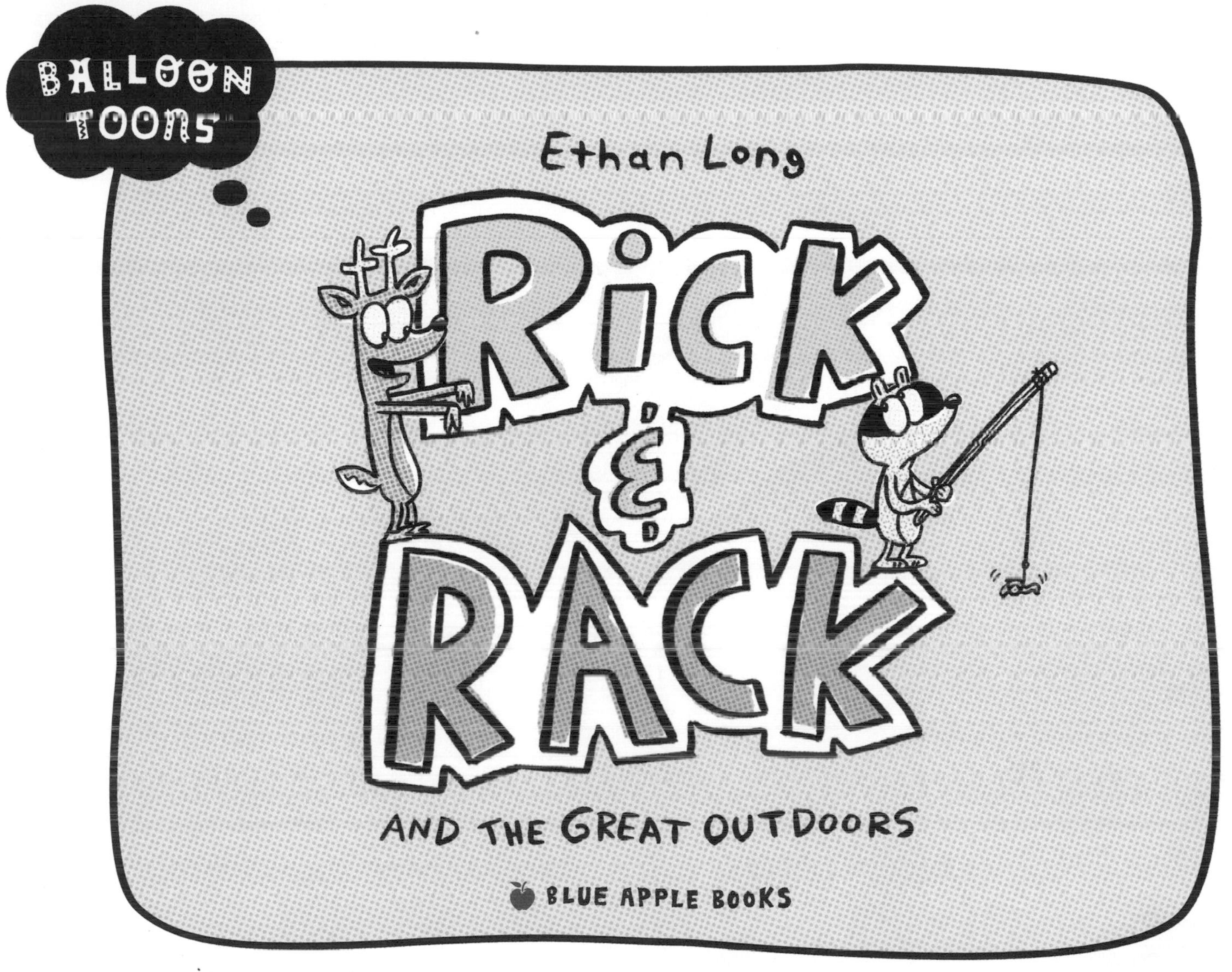

AND THE GREAT OUTDOORS

BLUE APPLE BOOKS

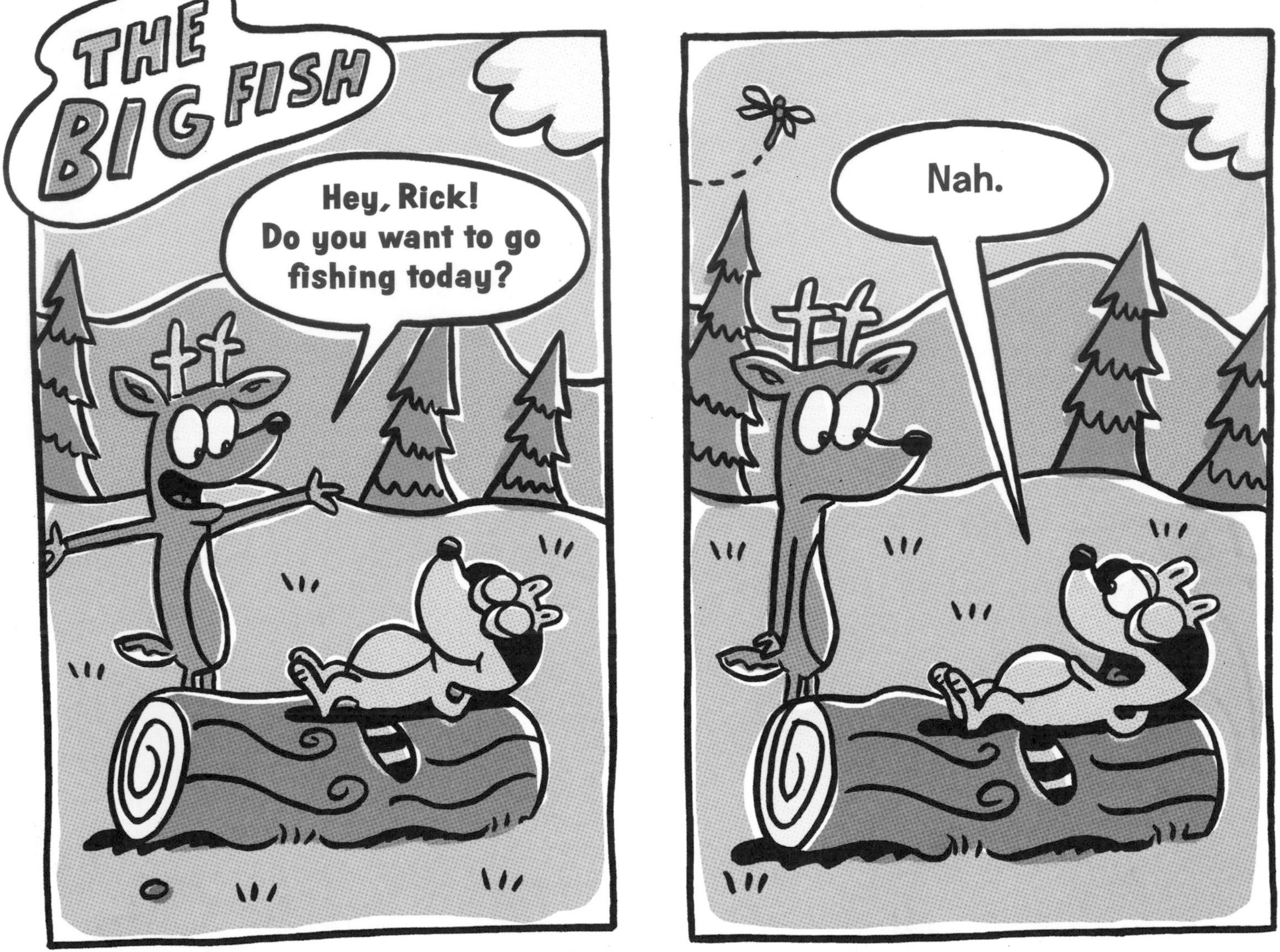
THE BIG FISH
Hey, Rick! Do you want to go fishing today?
Nah.

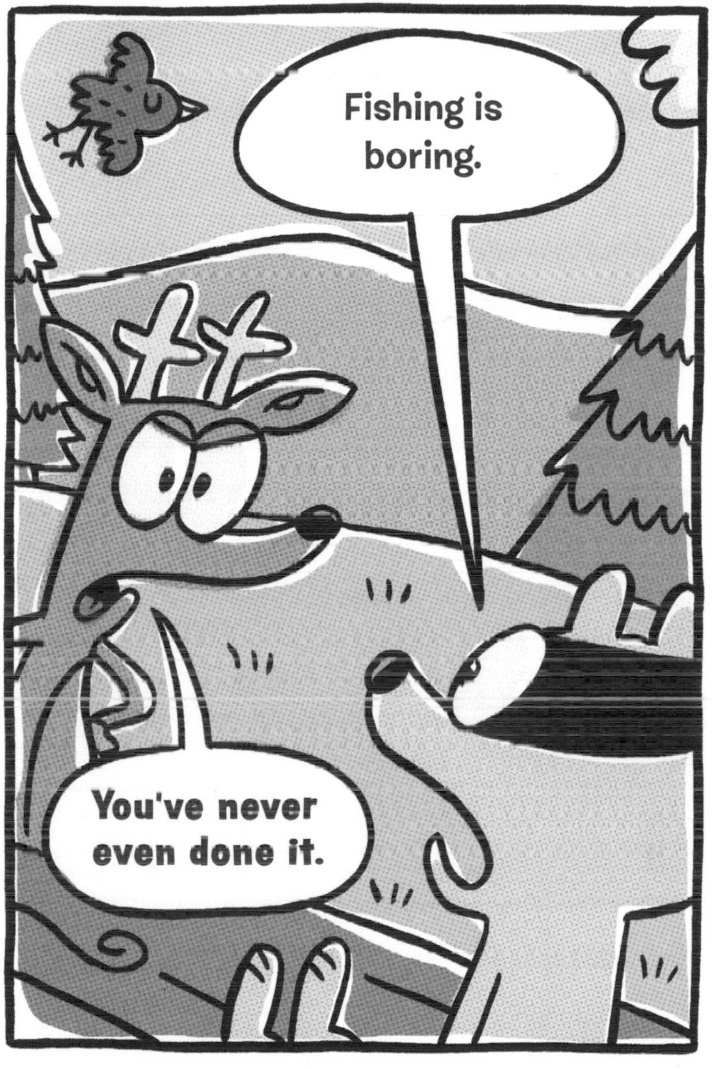
Fishing is boring.
You've never even done it.
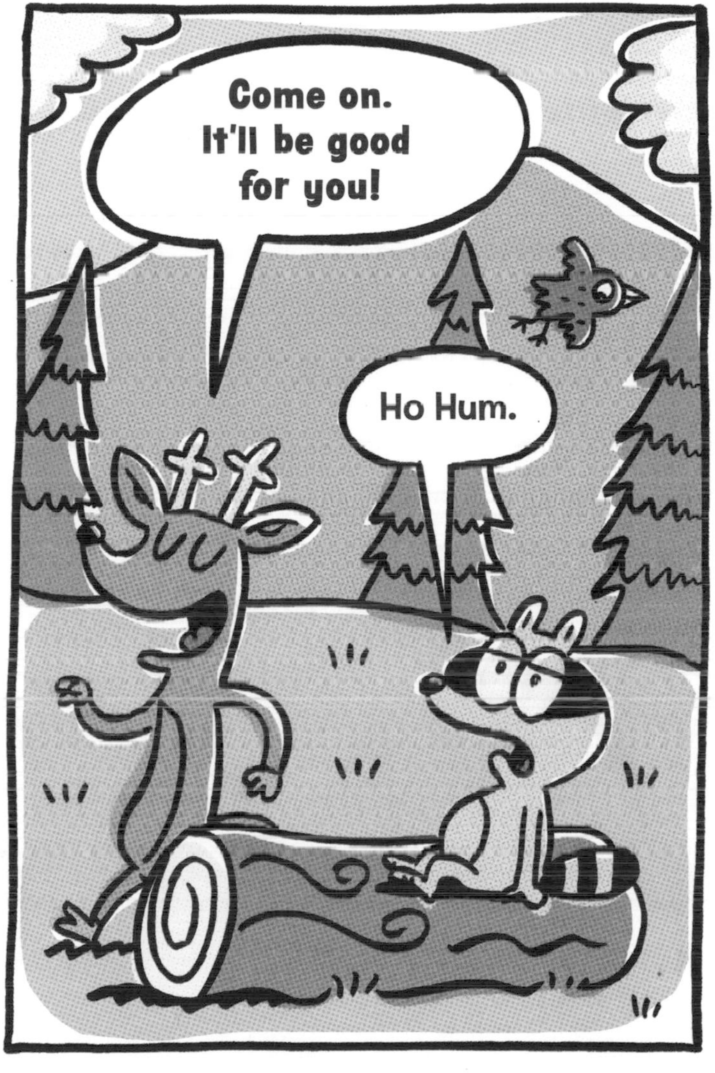
Come on. It'll be good for you!
Ho Hum.

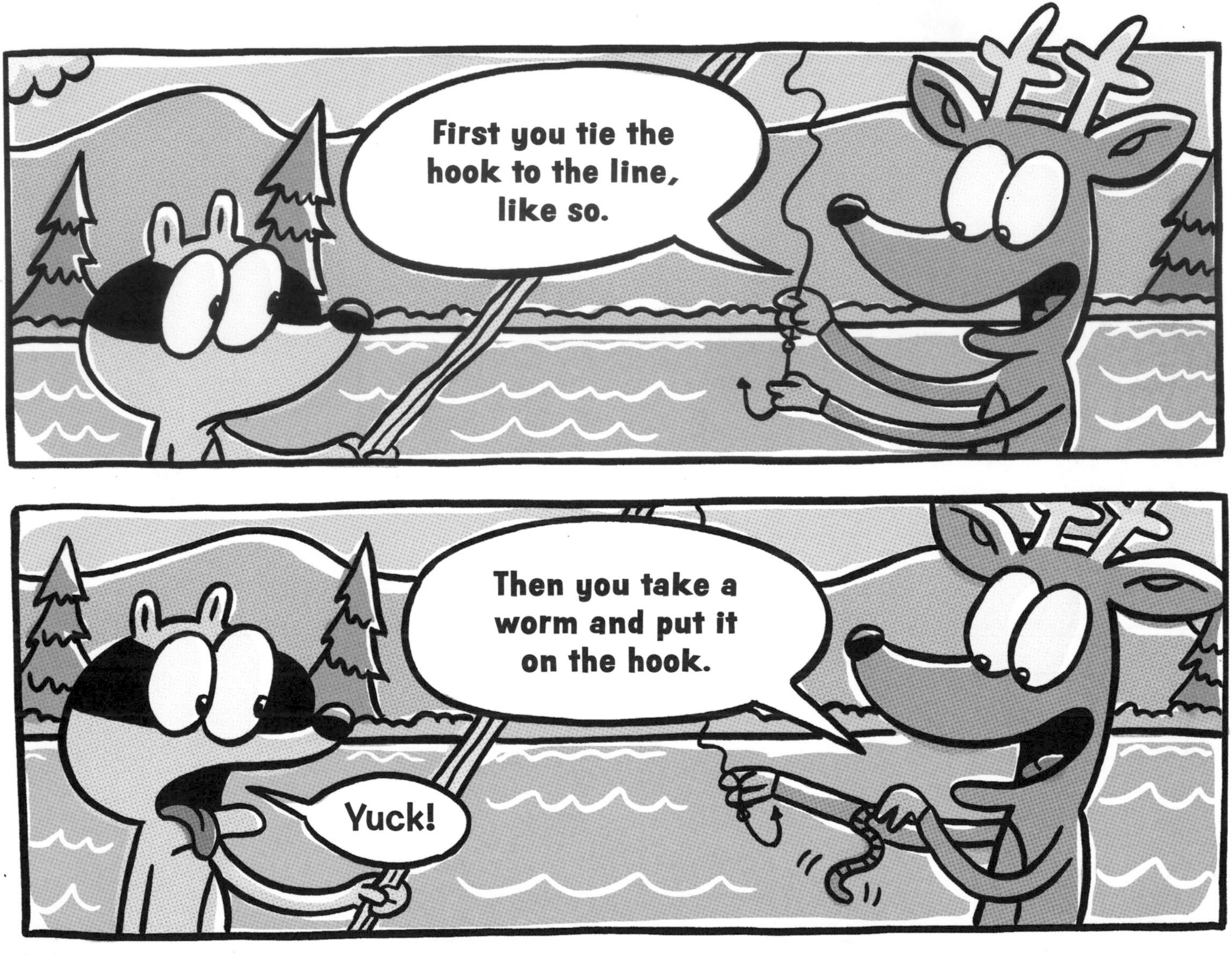
First you tie the hook to the line, like so.
Then you take a worm and put it on the hook.
Yuck!

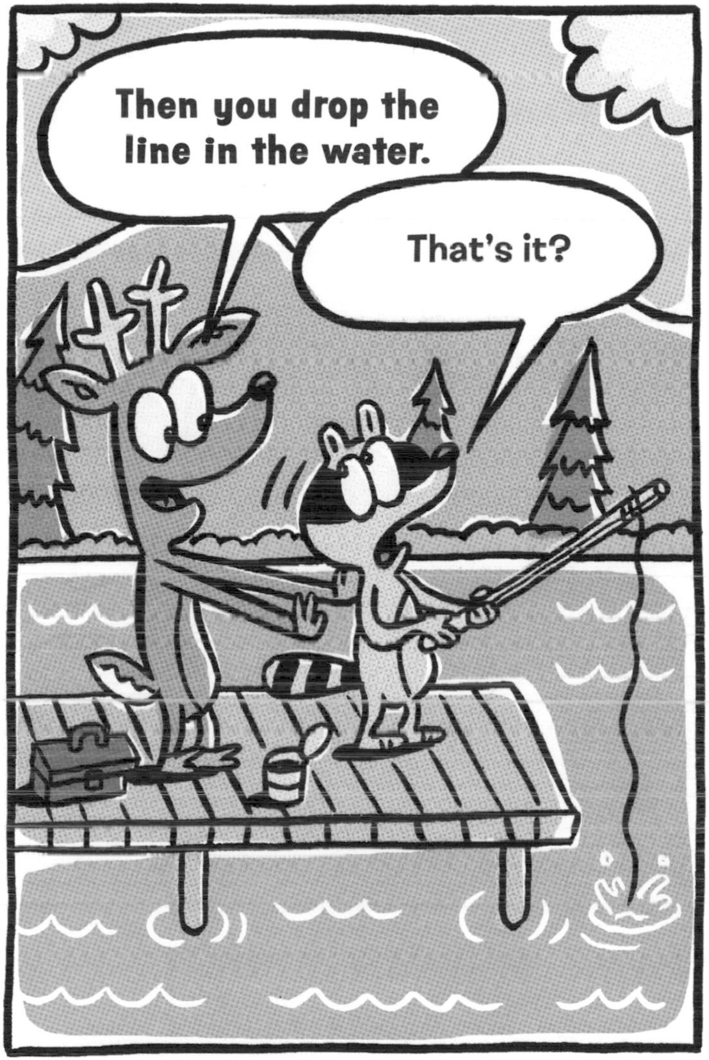
Then you drop the line in the water.
That's it?

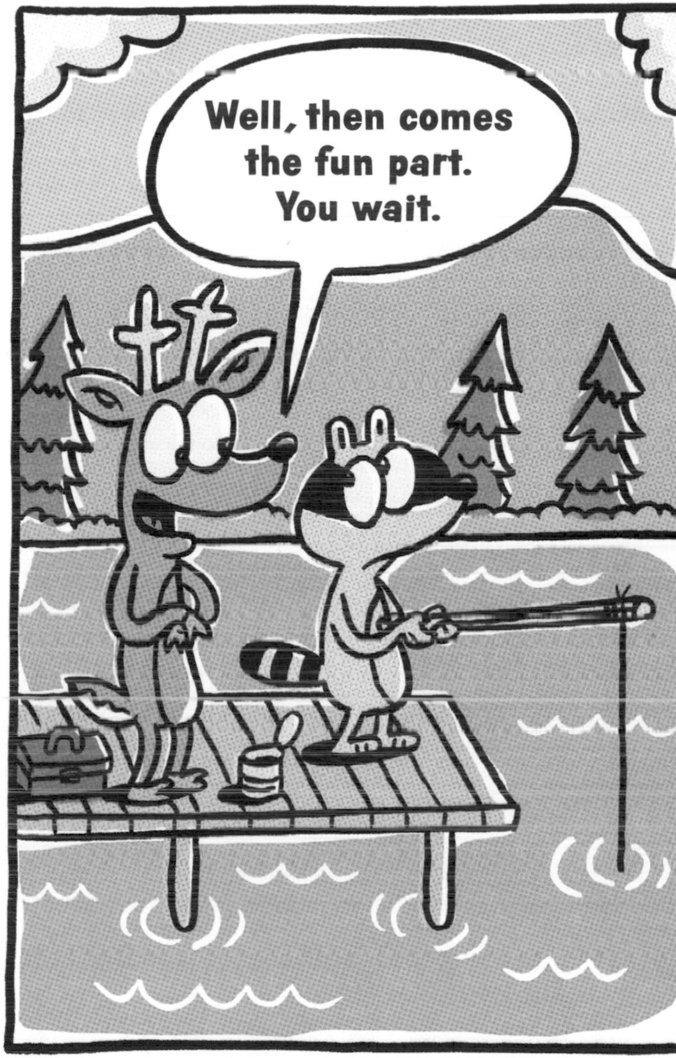
Well, then comes the fun part. You wait.

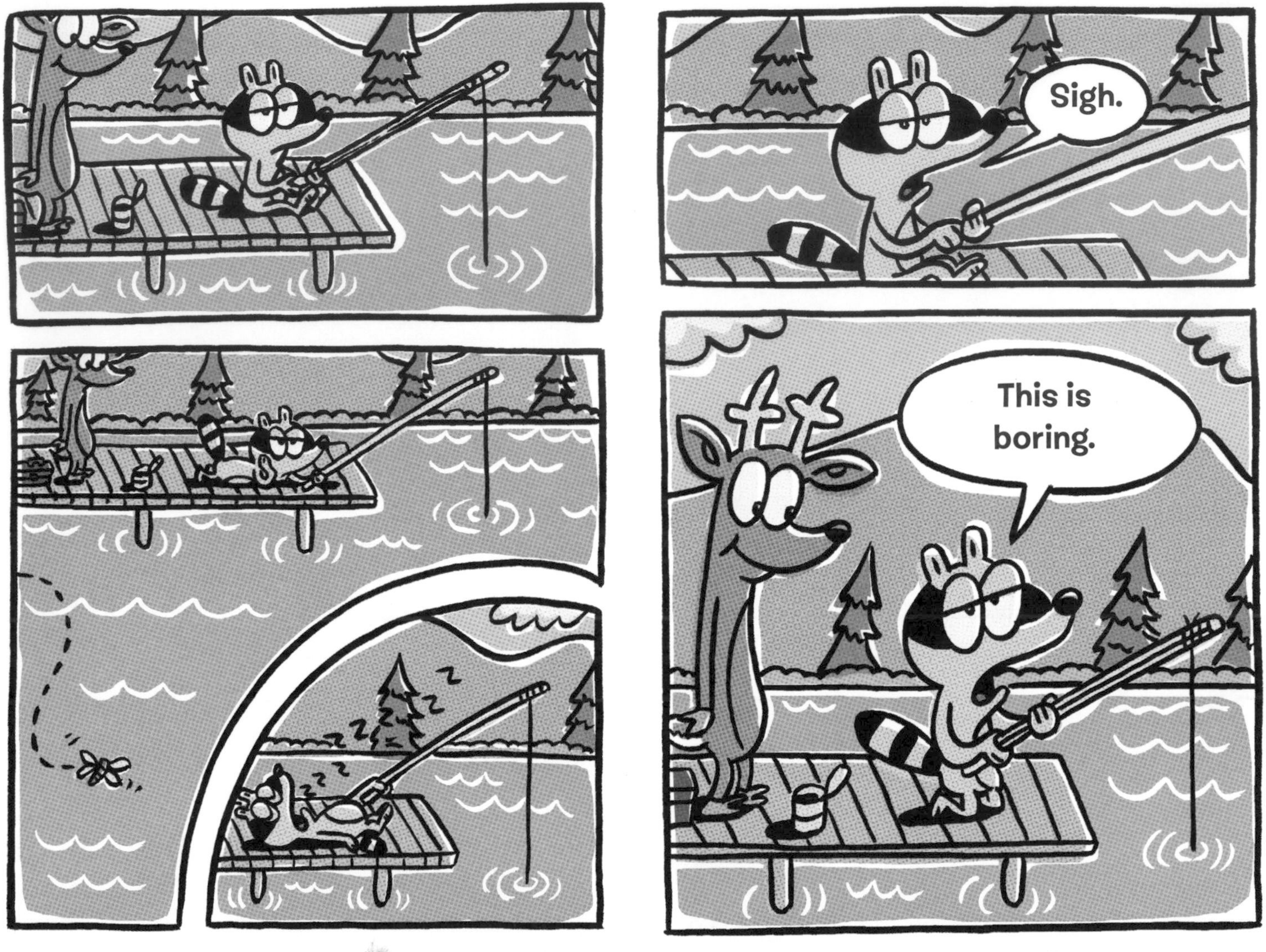
Sigh.
This is boring.

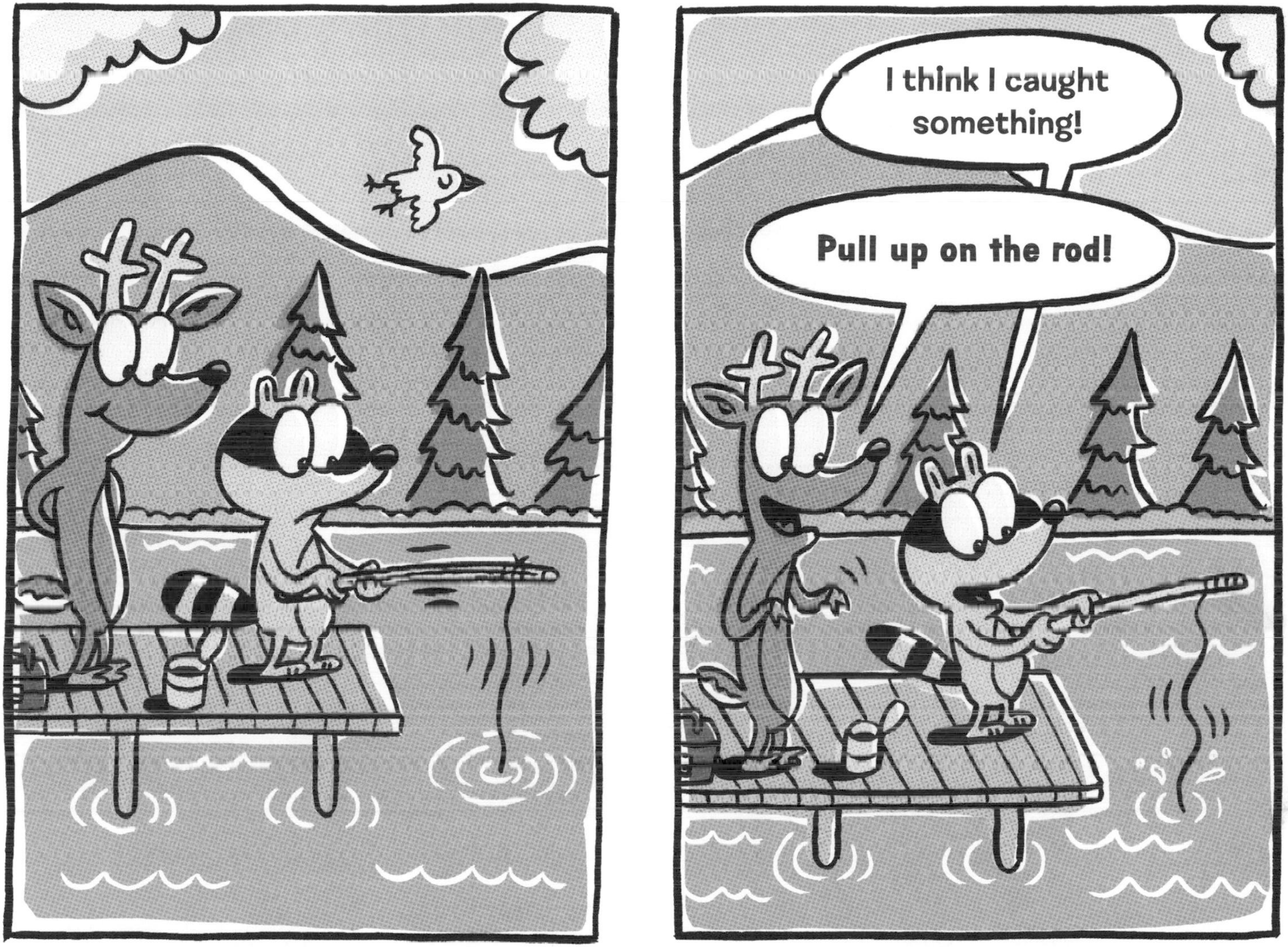
I think I caught something!
Pull up on the rod!

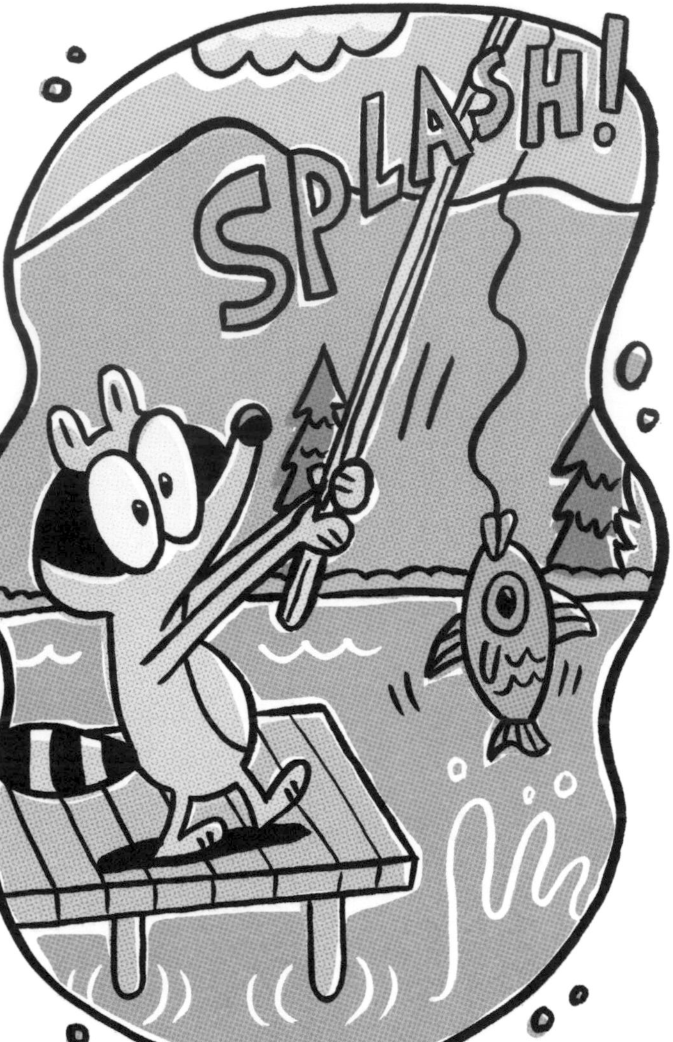
SPLASH!

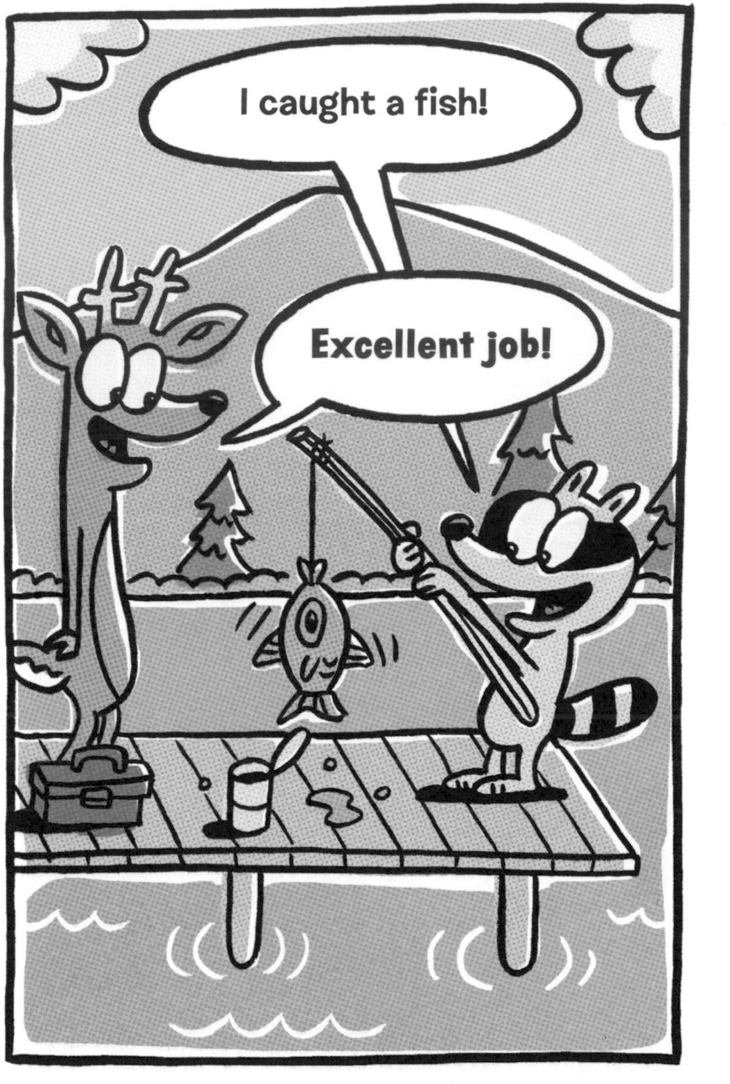
I caught a fish!
Excellent job!

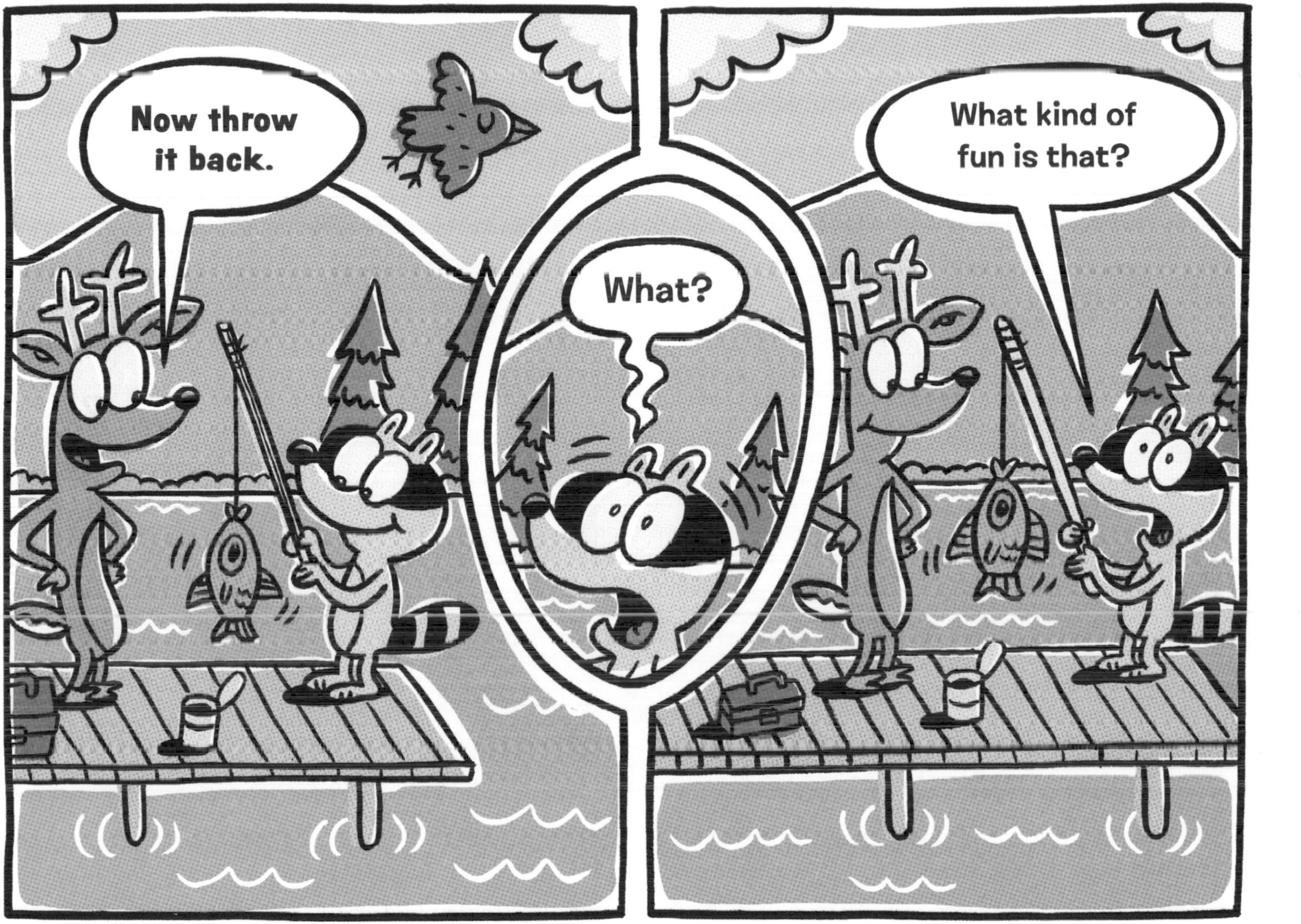
Now throw it back.
What?
What kind of fun is that?

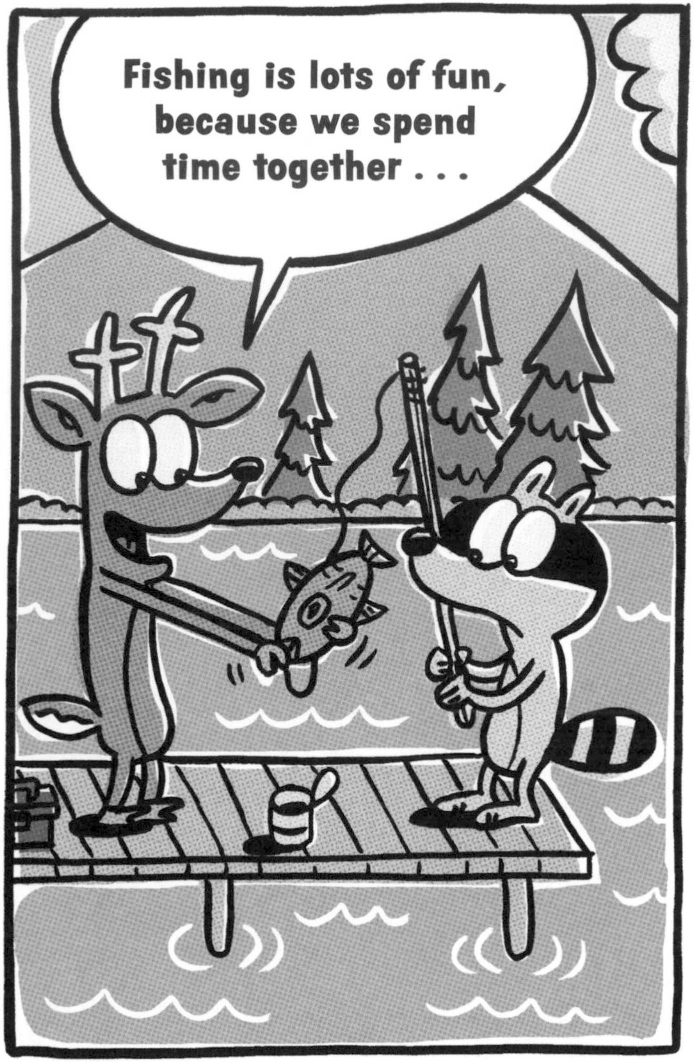
Fishing is lots of fun, because we spend time together . . .

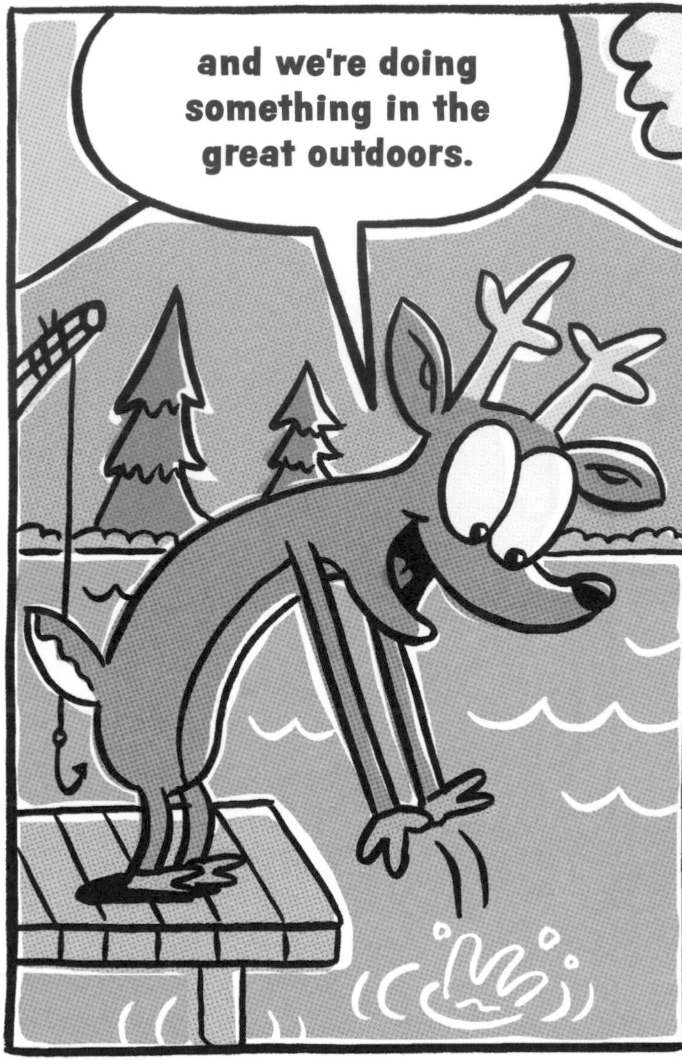
and we're doing something in the great outdoors.

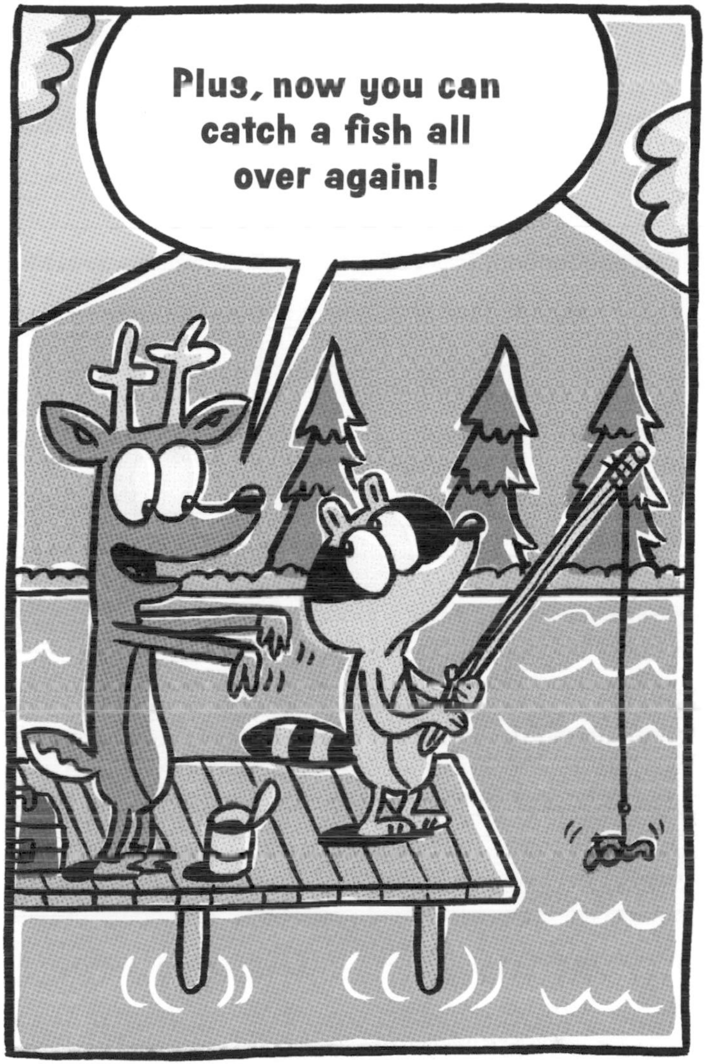
Plus, now you can catch a fish all over again!

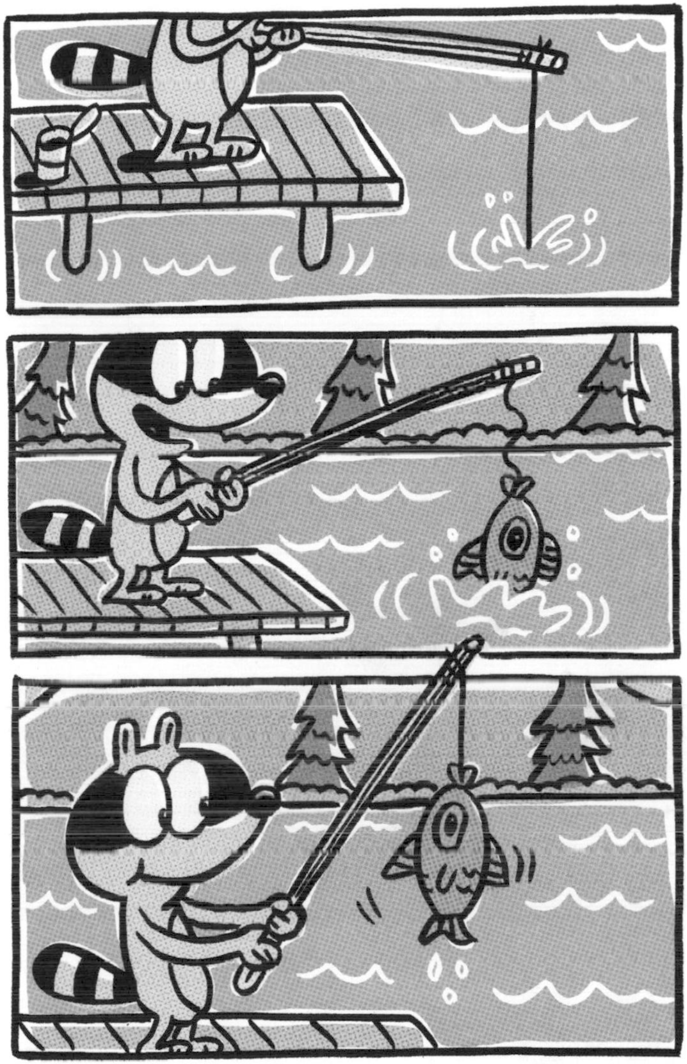

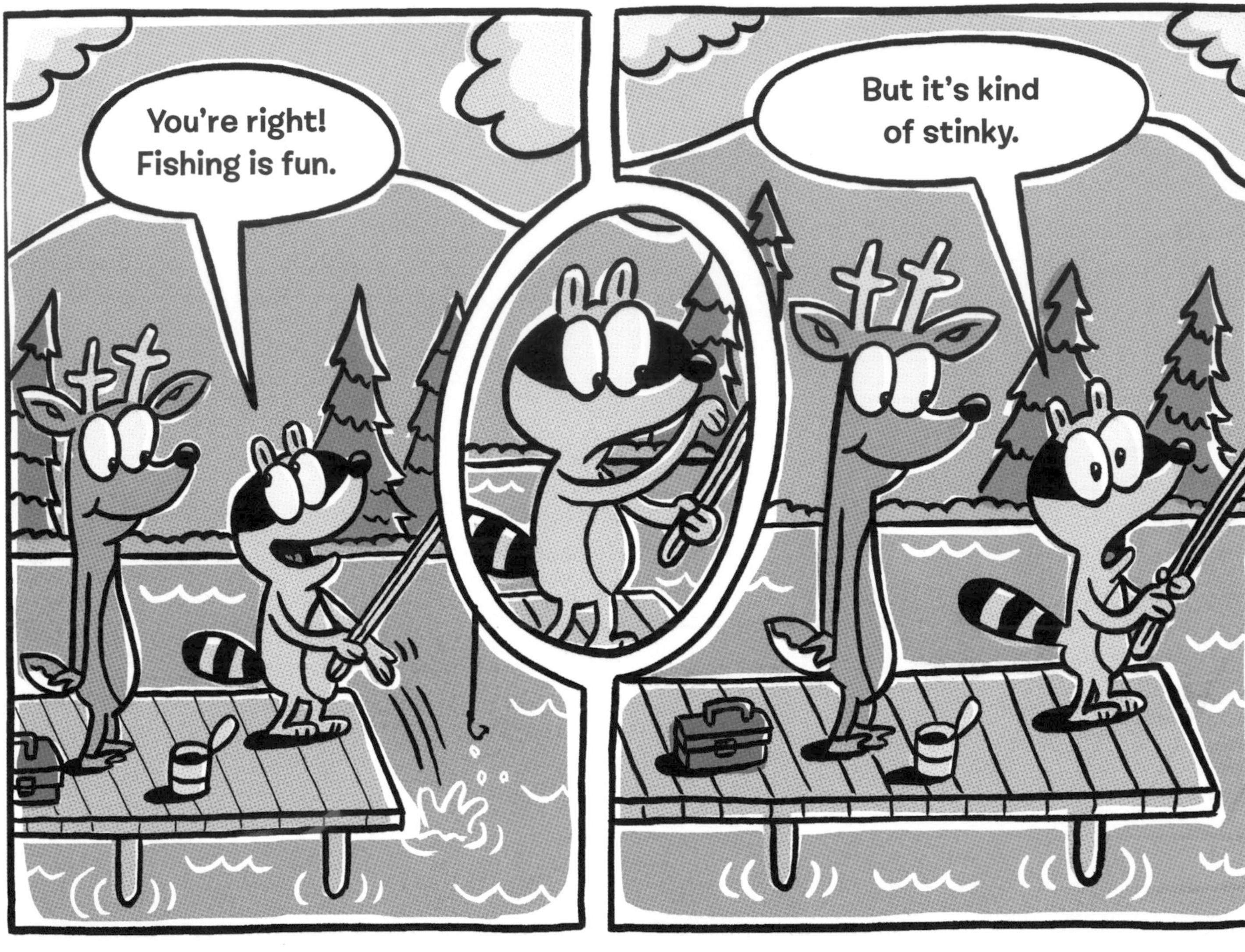
You're right!
Fishing is fun.
But it's kind
of stinky.

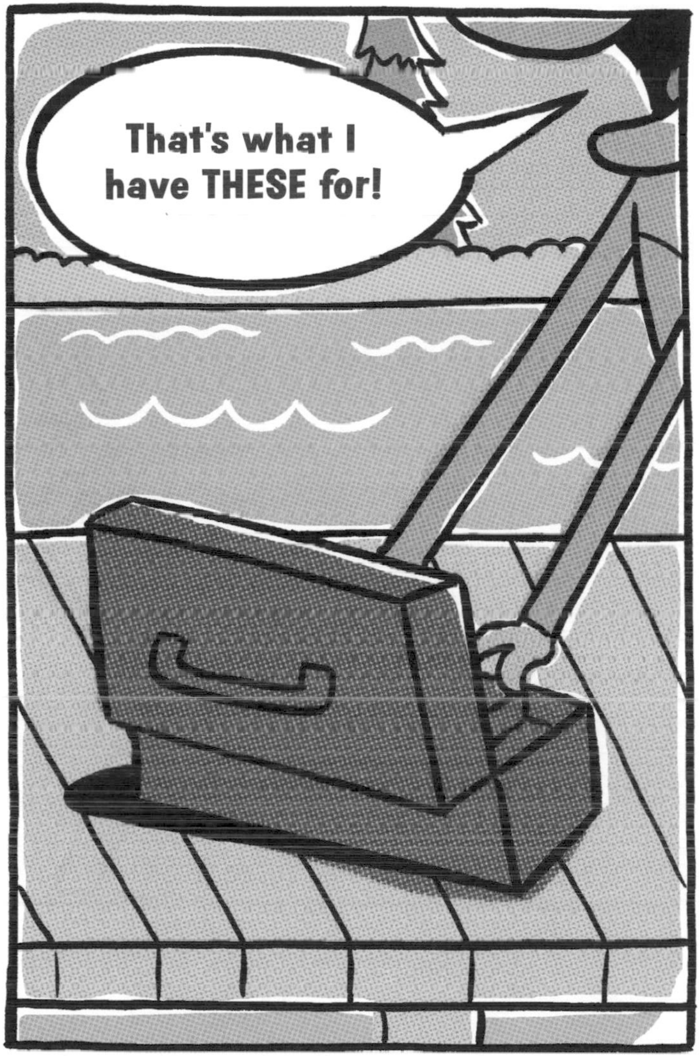
That's what I have THESE for!

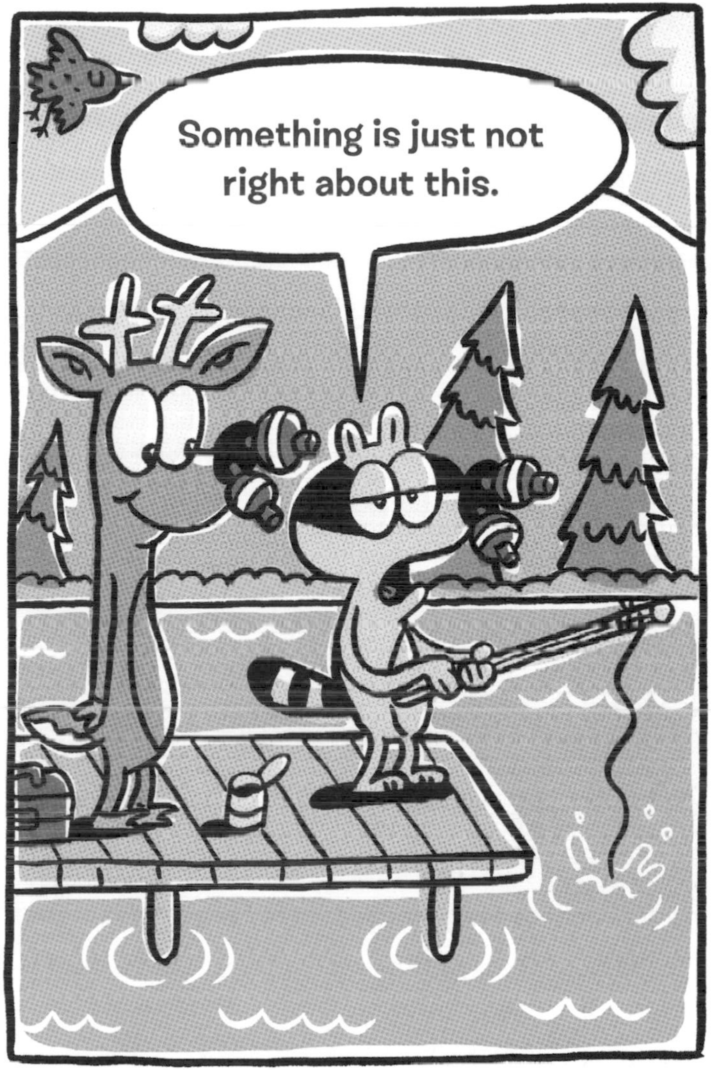
Something is just not right about this.

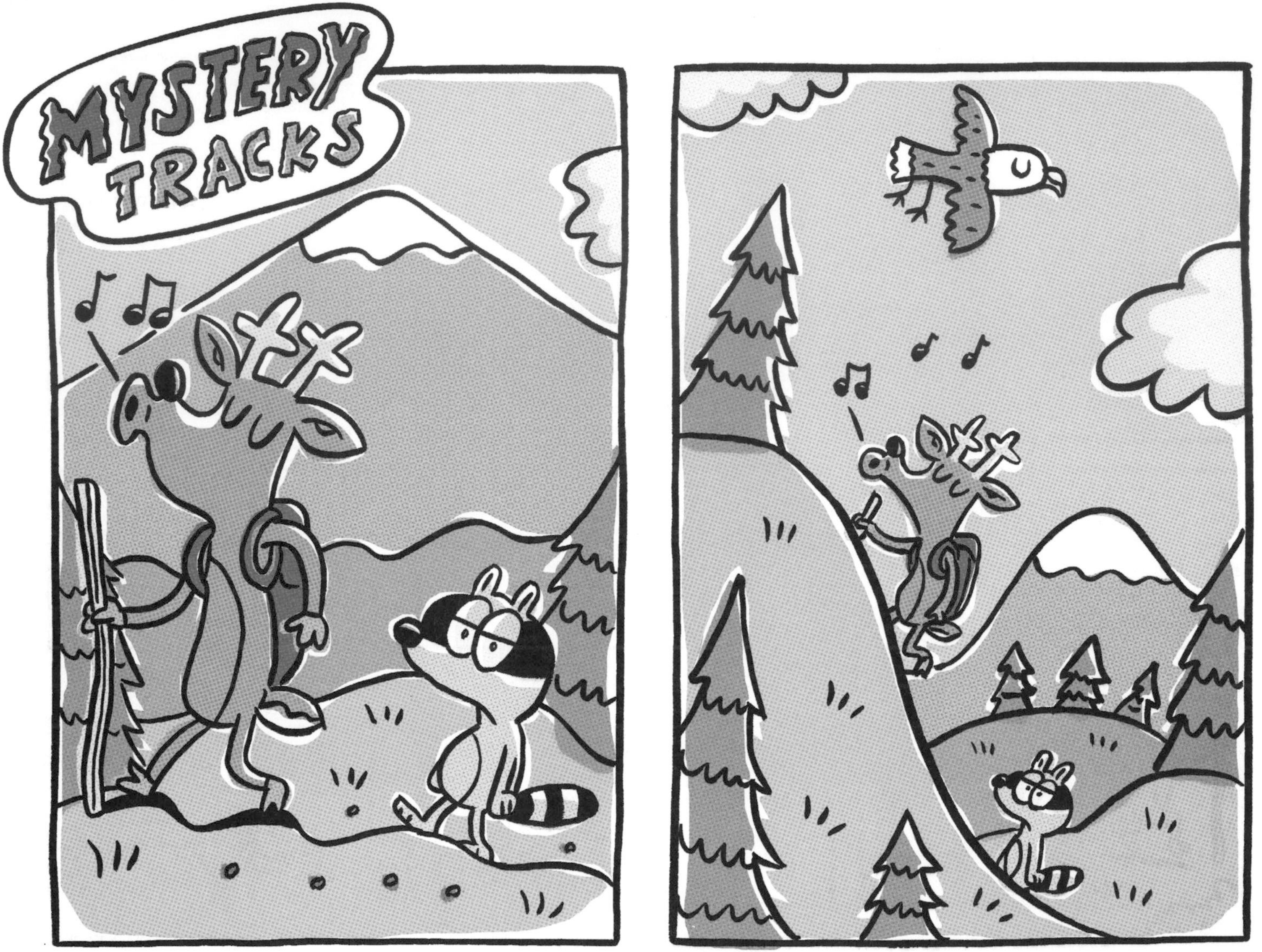
MYSTERY TRACKS

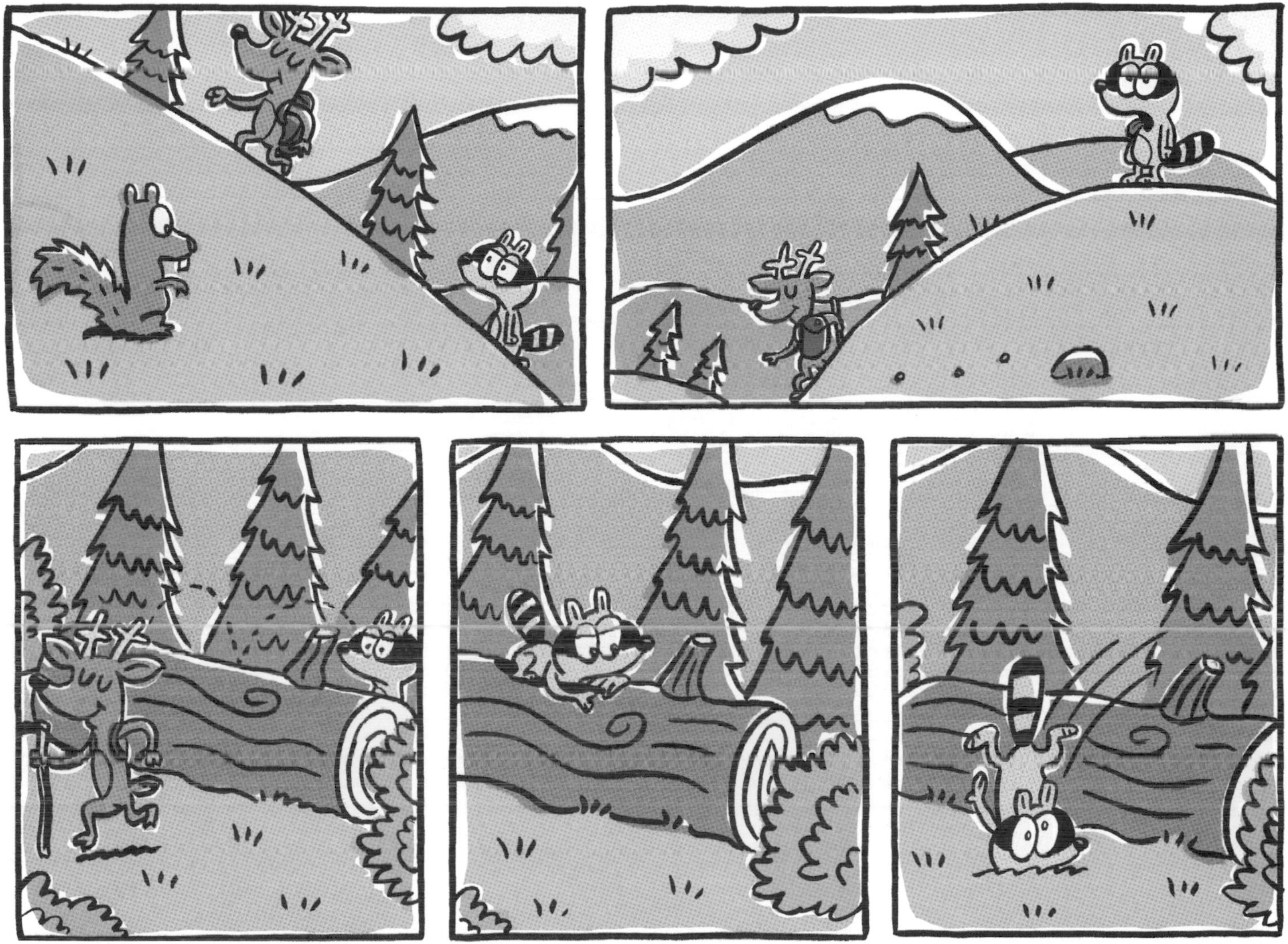

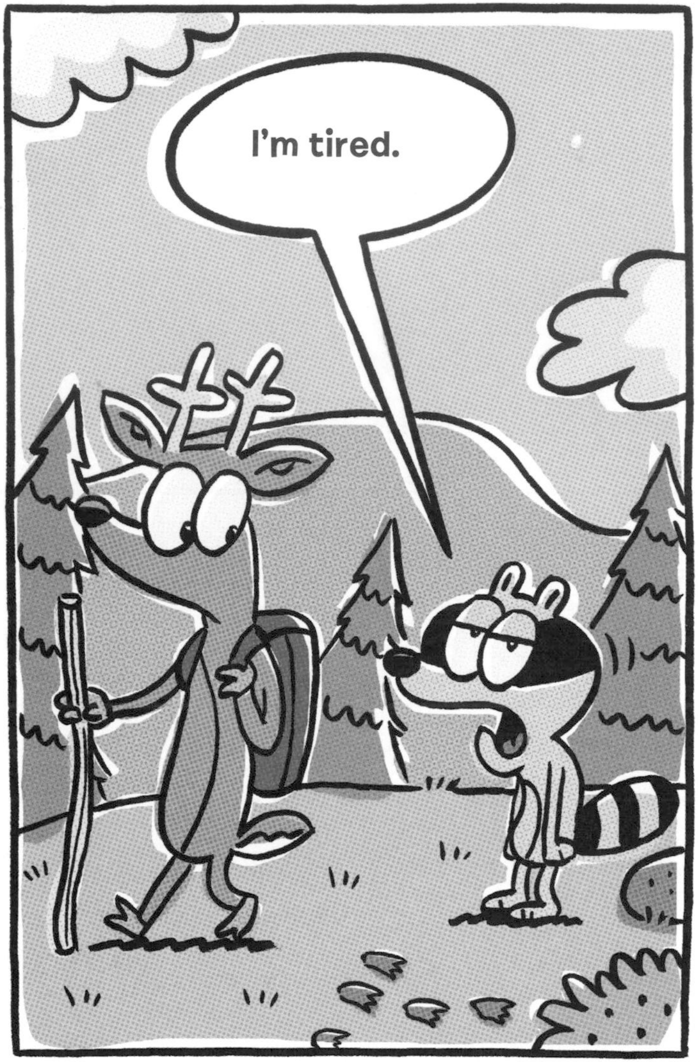
I'm tired.

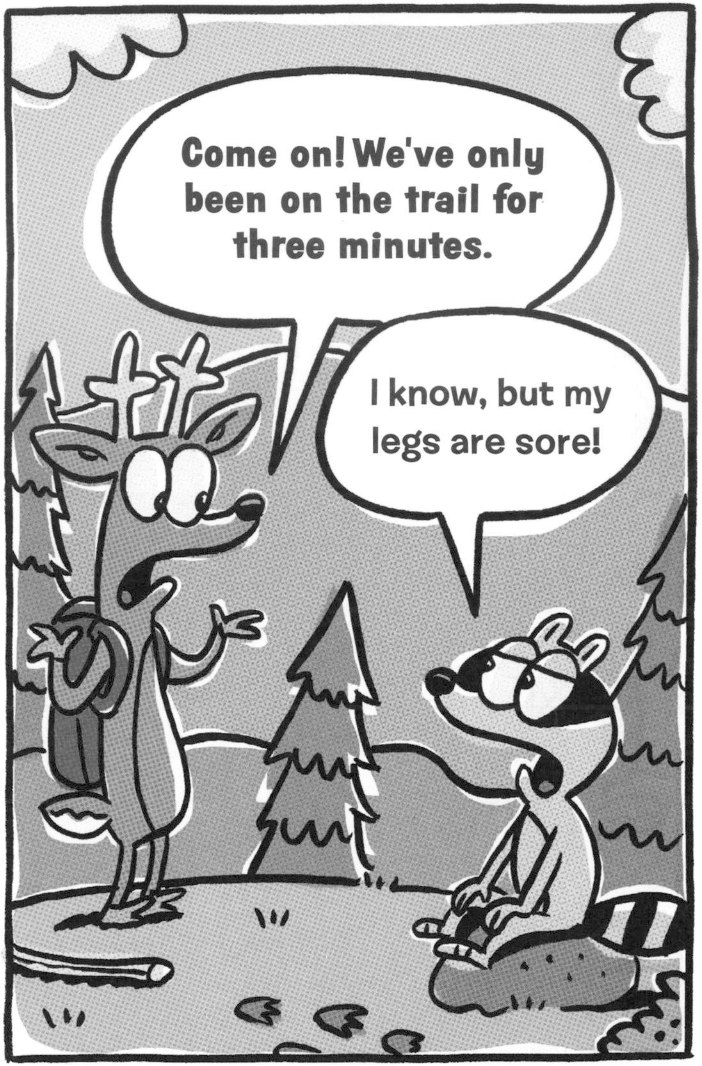
Come on! We've only been on the trail for three minutes.
I know, but my legs are sore!

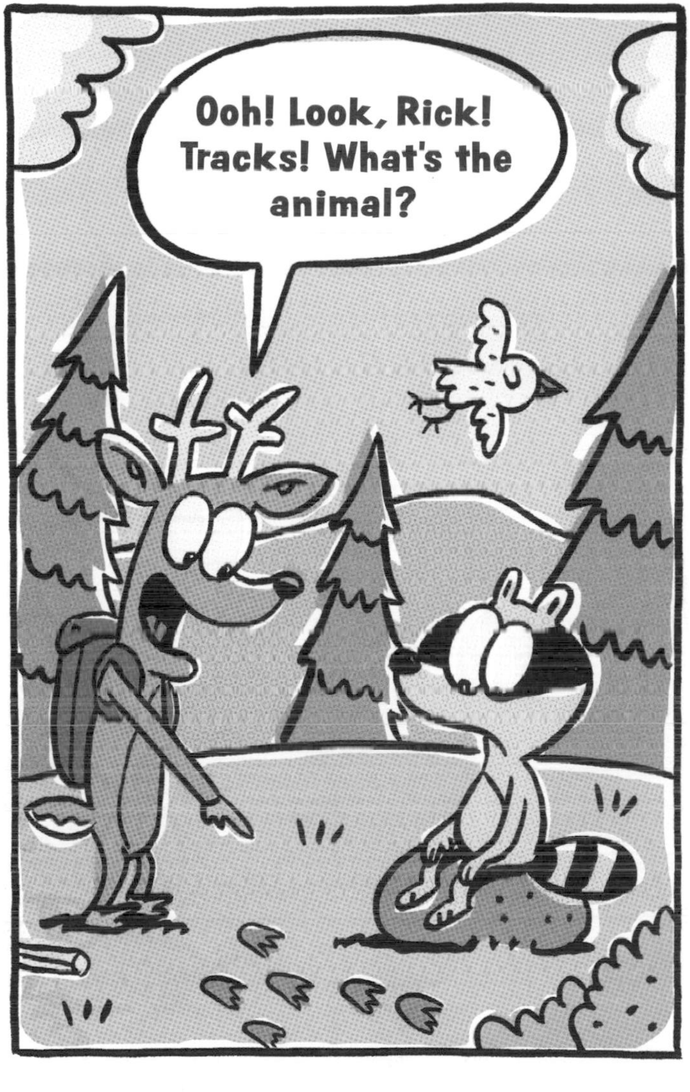
Ooh! Look, Rick! Tracks! What's the animal?

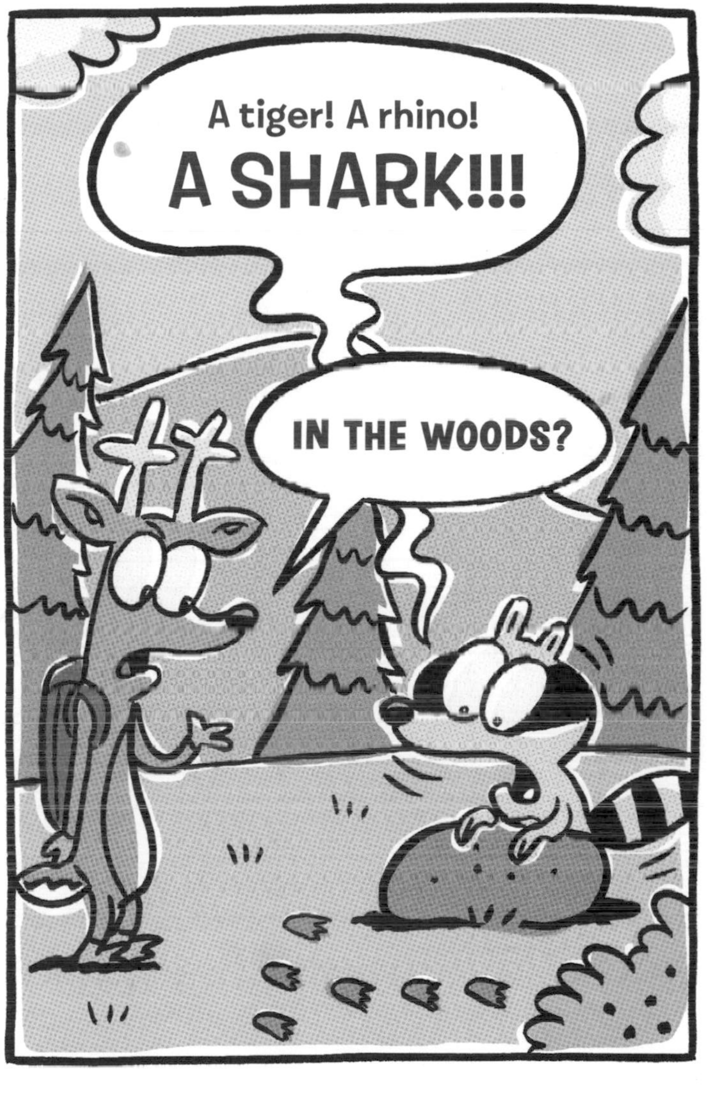
A tiger! A rhino!
A SHARK!!!
IN THE WOODS?

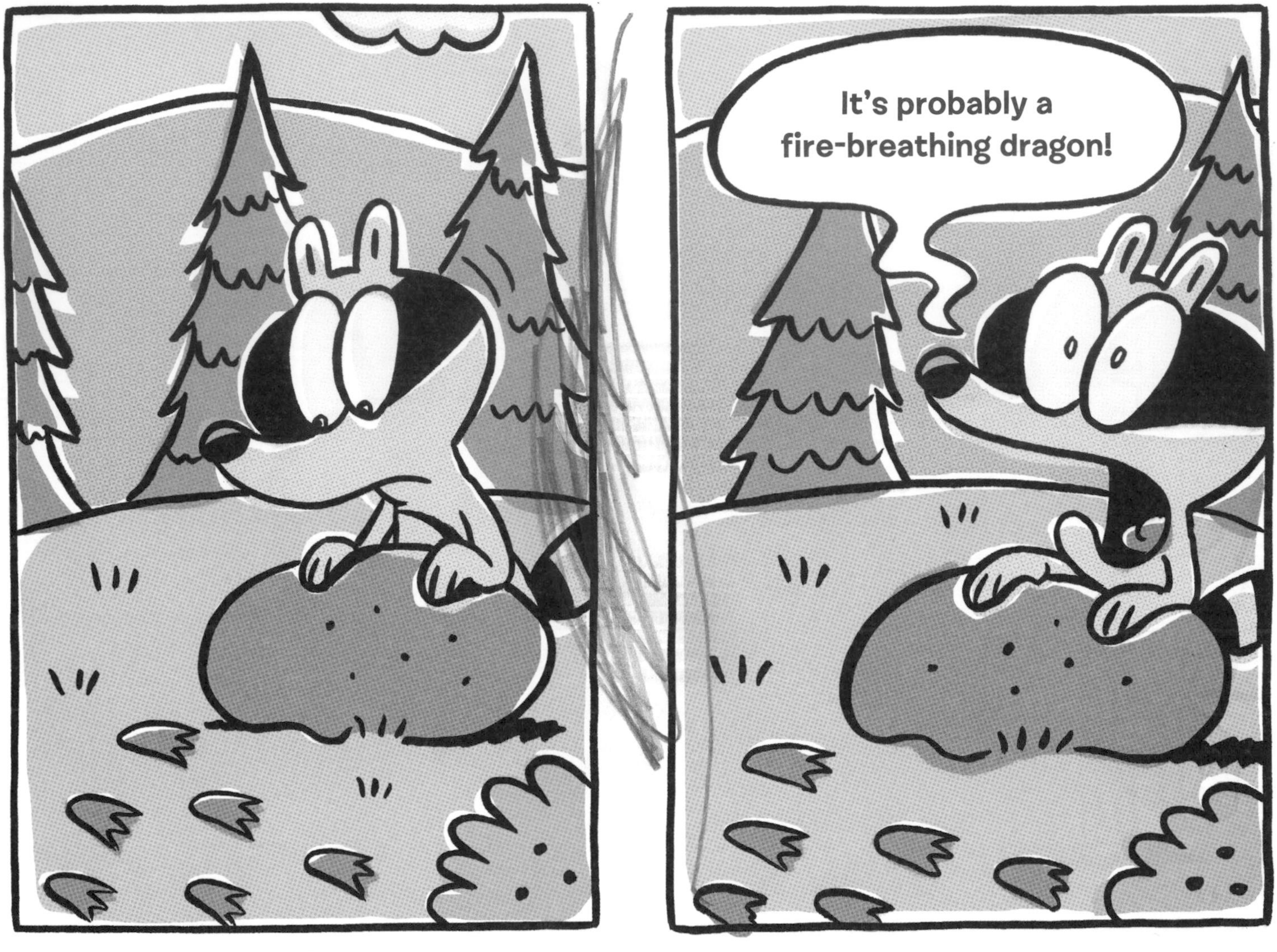
It's probably a fire-breathing dragon!

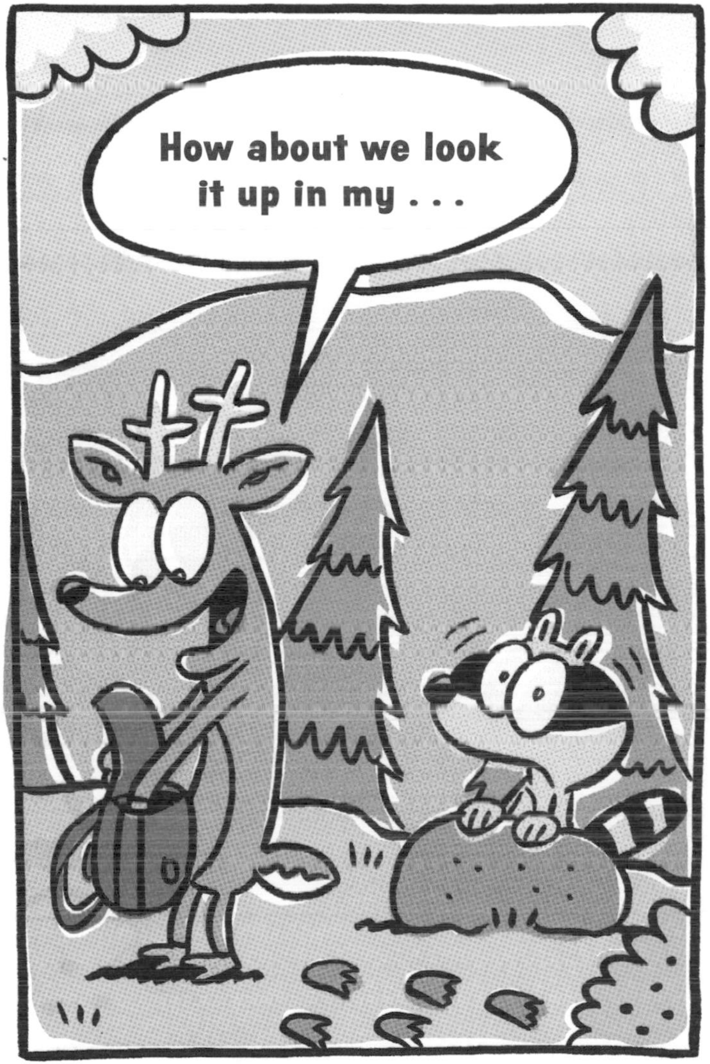
How about we look it up in my . . .

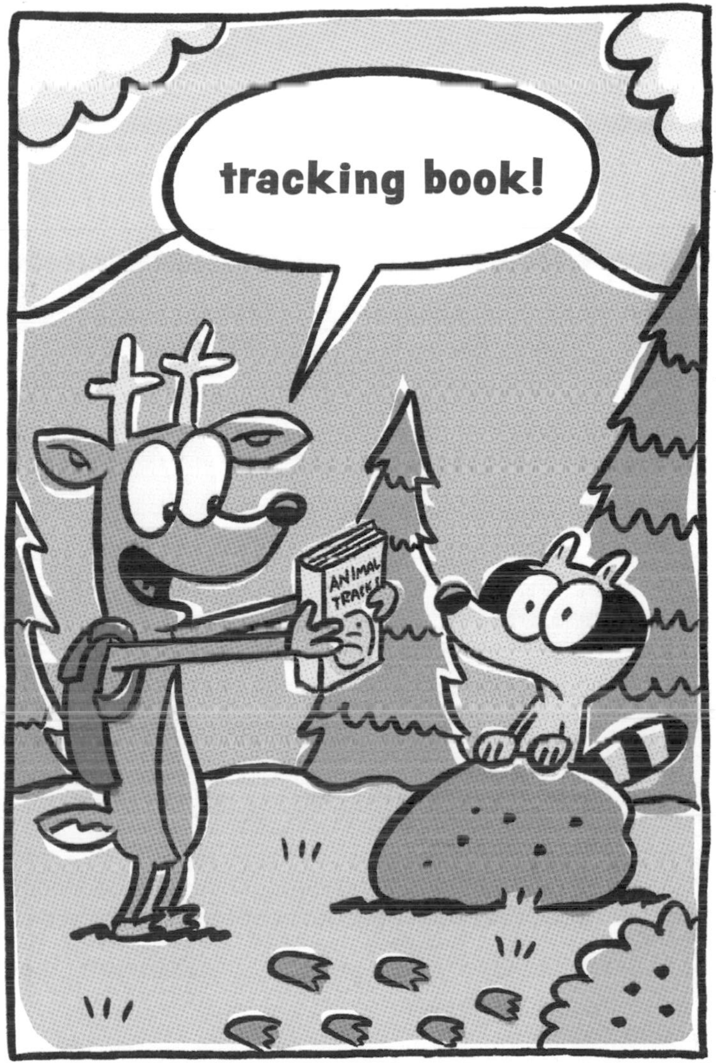
tracking book!
ANIMAL TRACKS

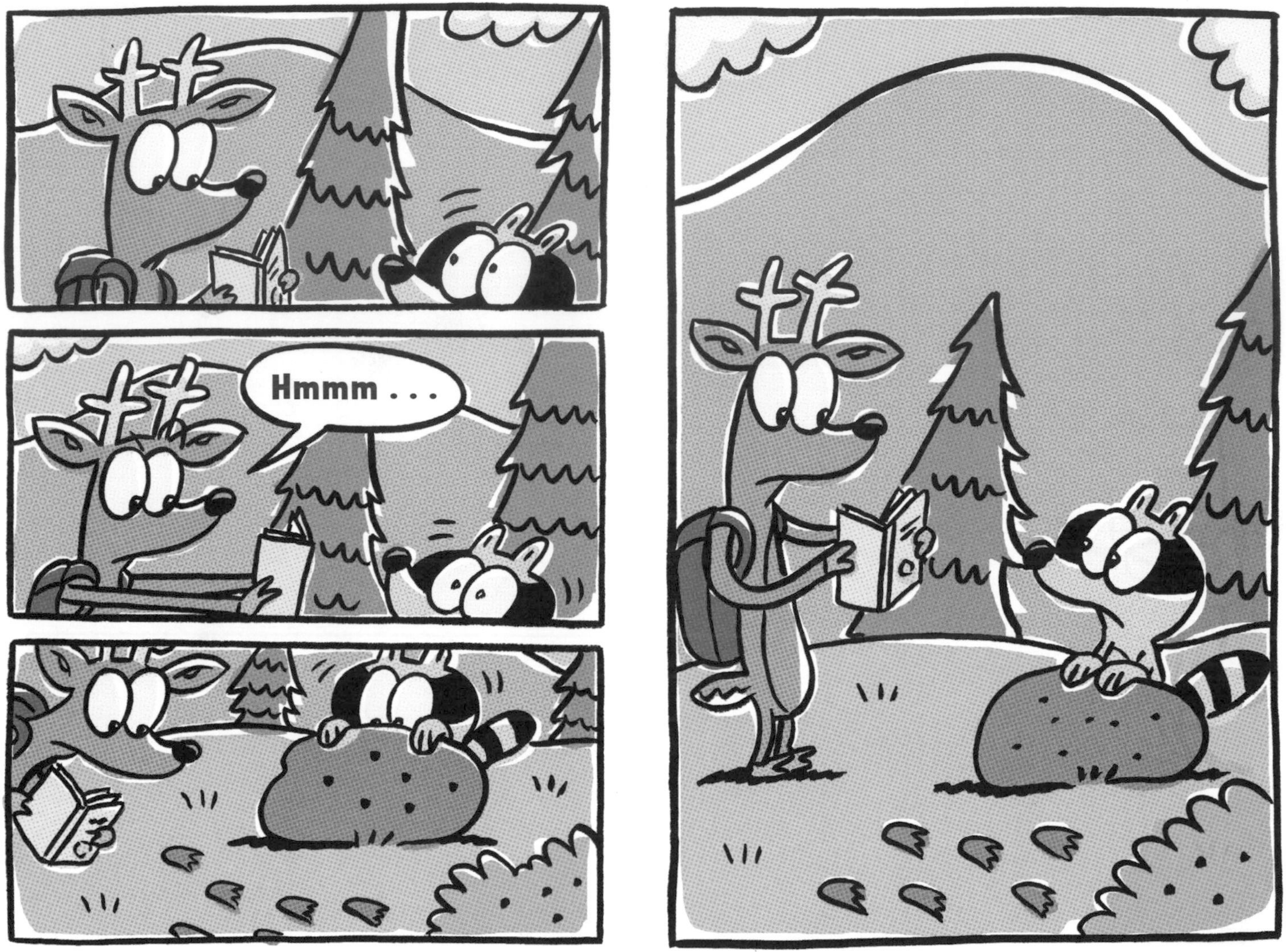
Hmmm . . .

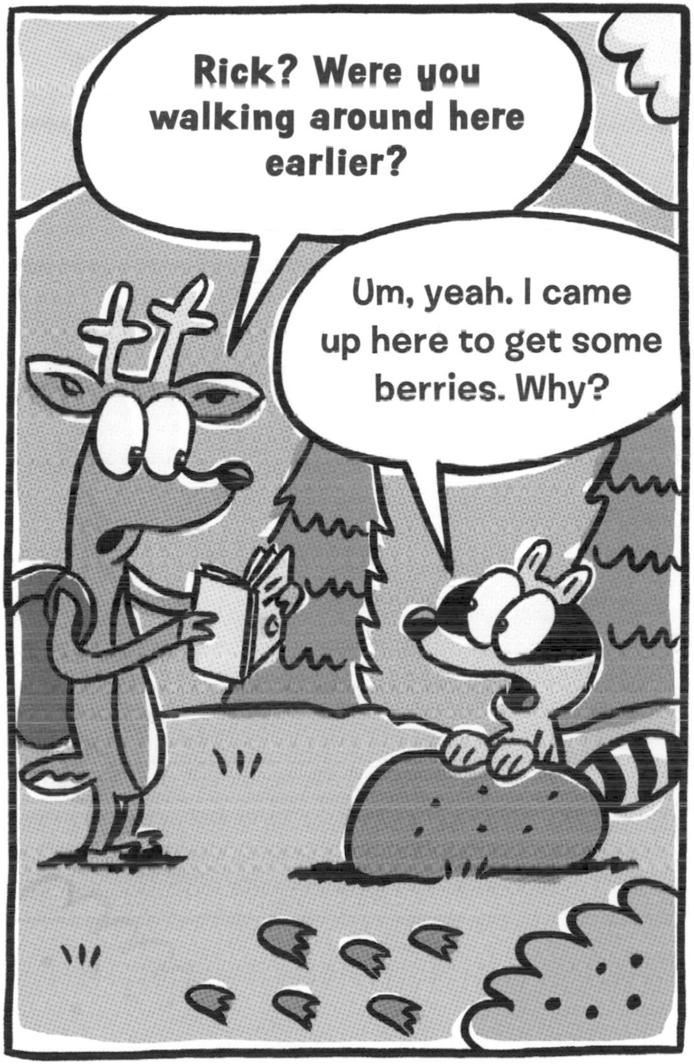
Rick? Were you walking around here earlier?
Um, yeah. I came up here to get some berries. Why?

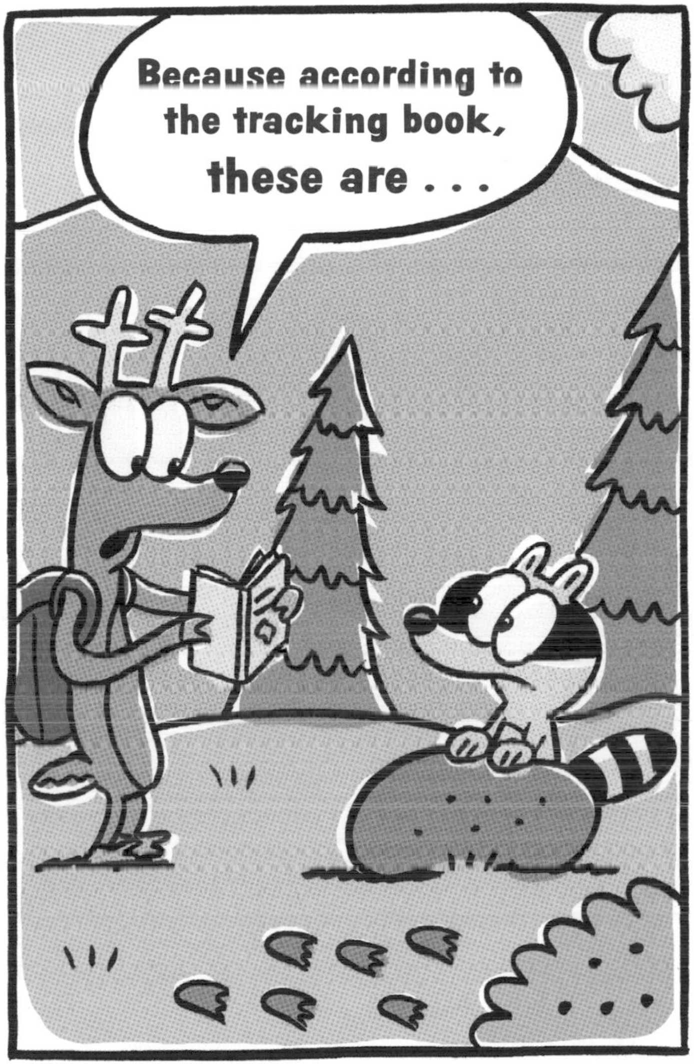
Because according to the tracking book, these are . . .

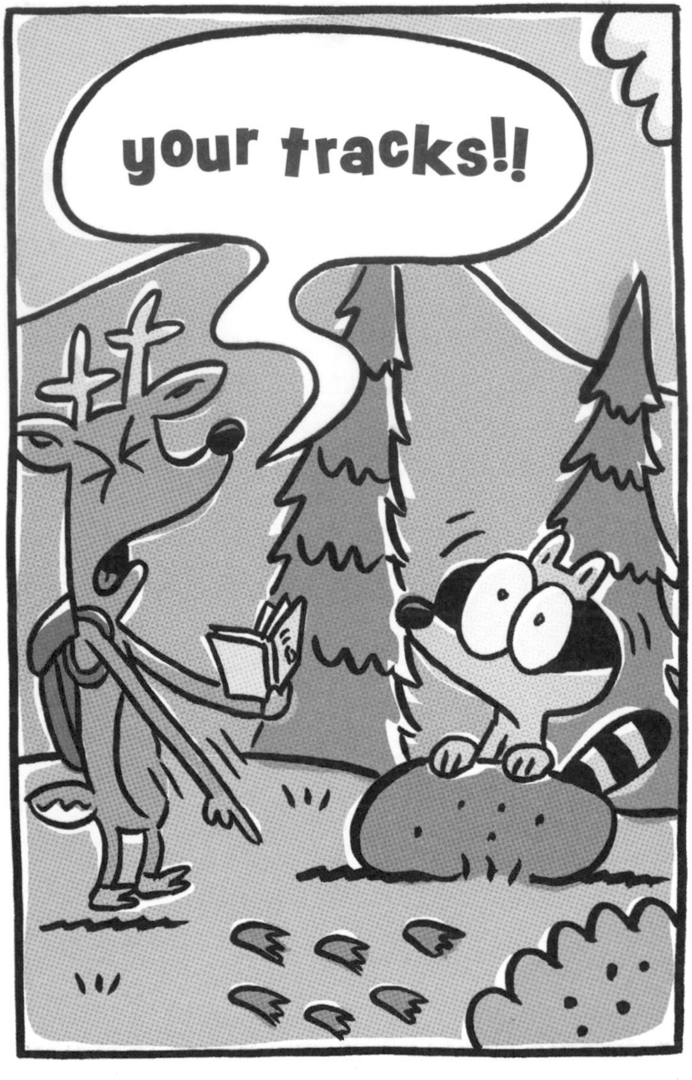
your tracks!!

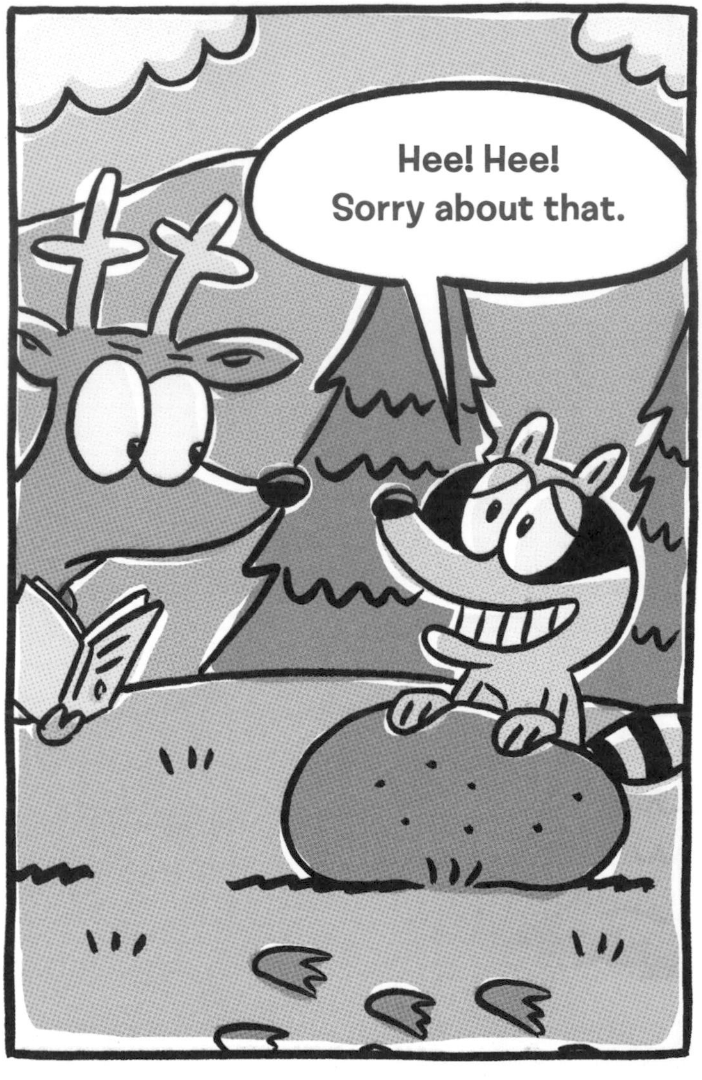
Hee! Hee!
Sorry about that.

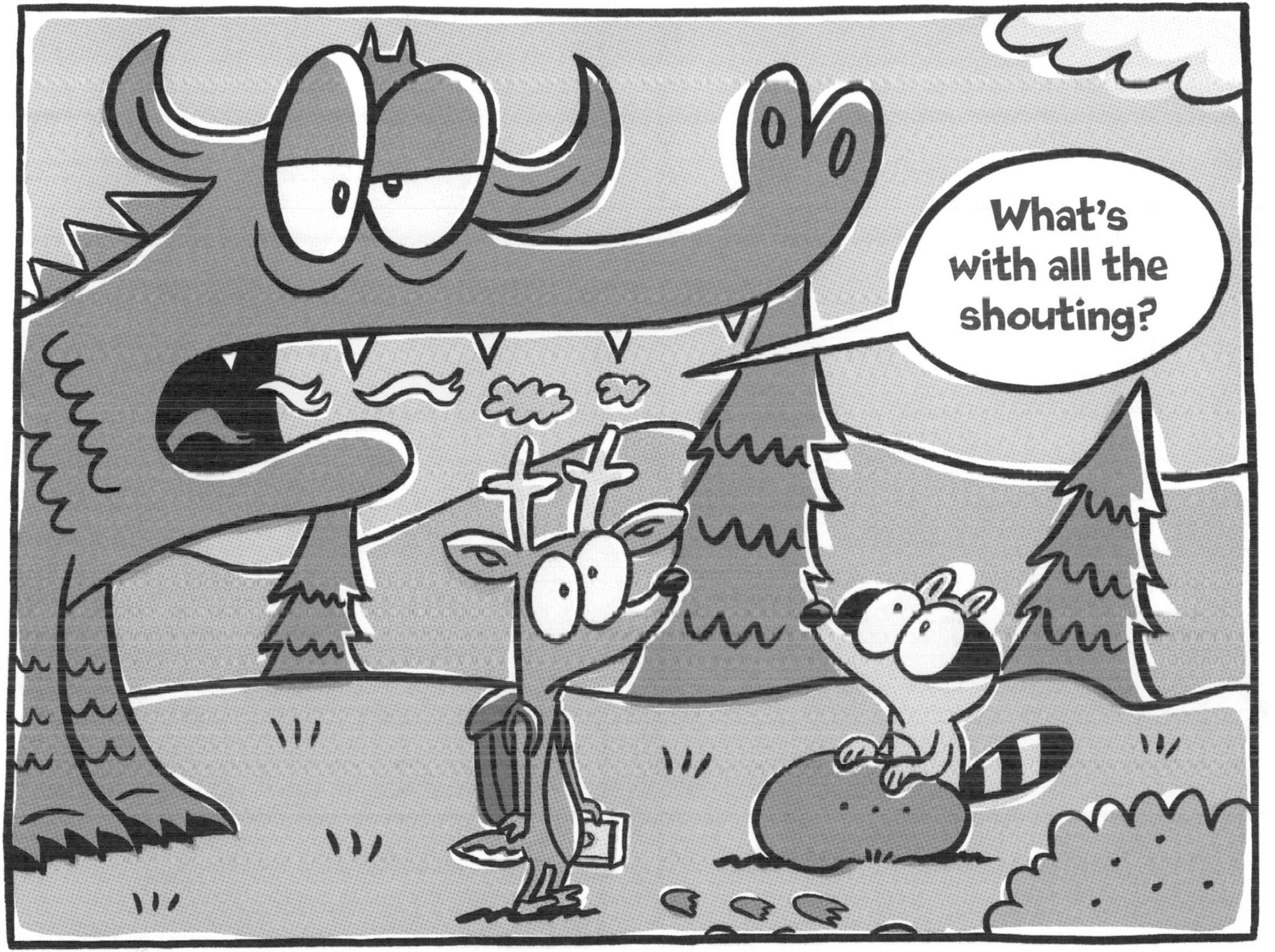
What's with all the shouting?

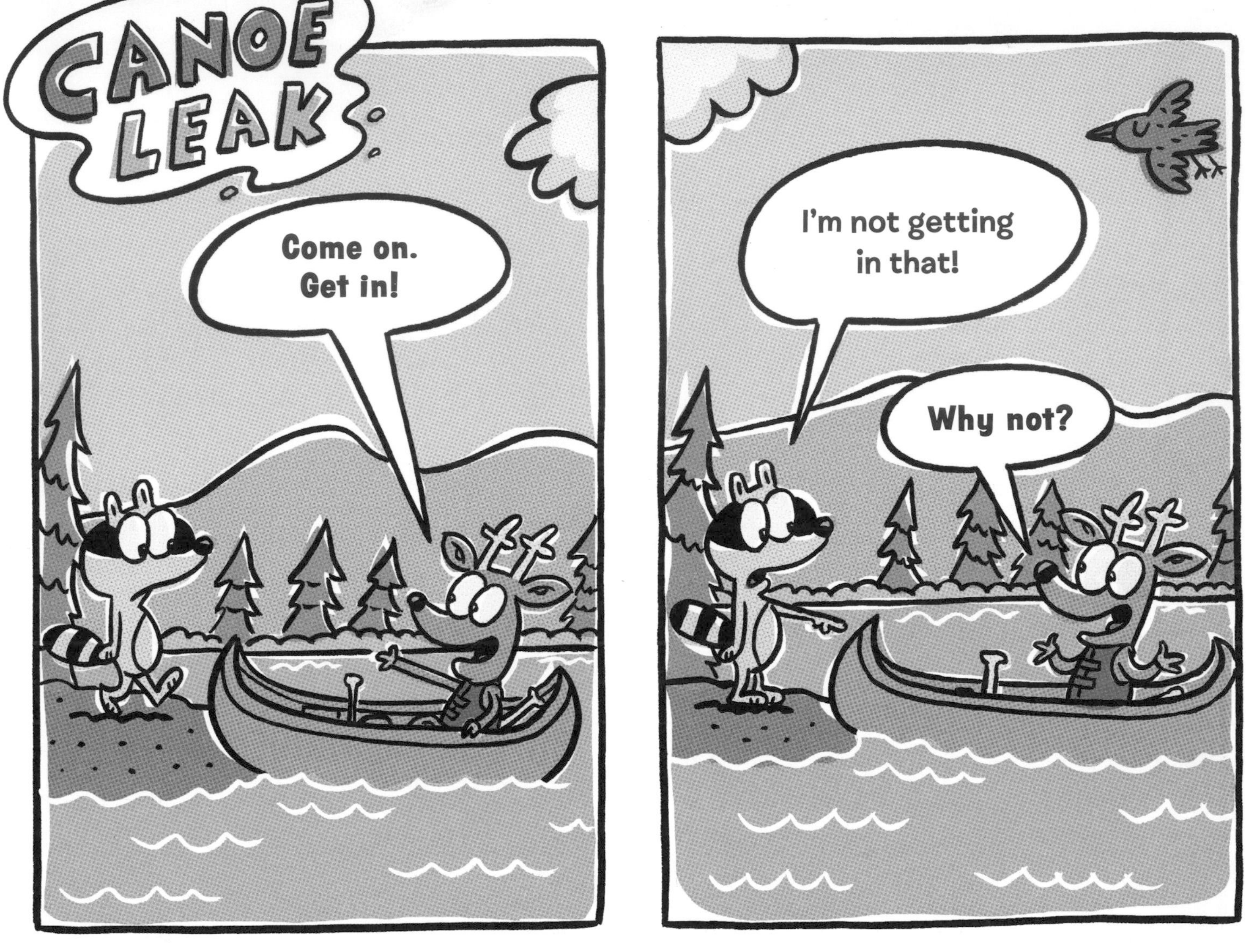
CANOE LEAK
Come on. Get in!
I'm not getting in that!
Why not?

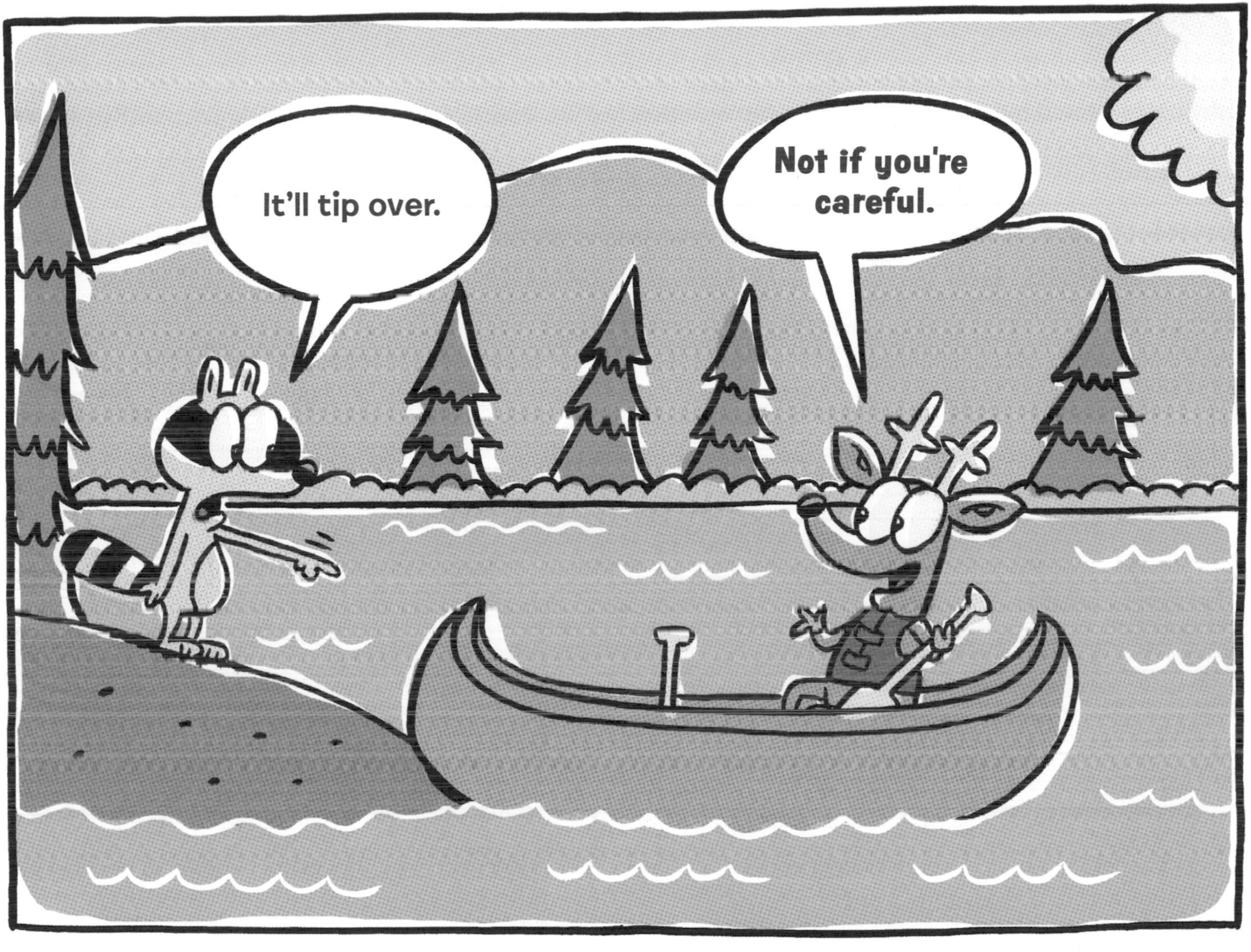
It'll tip over.
Not if you're careful.

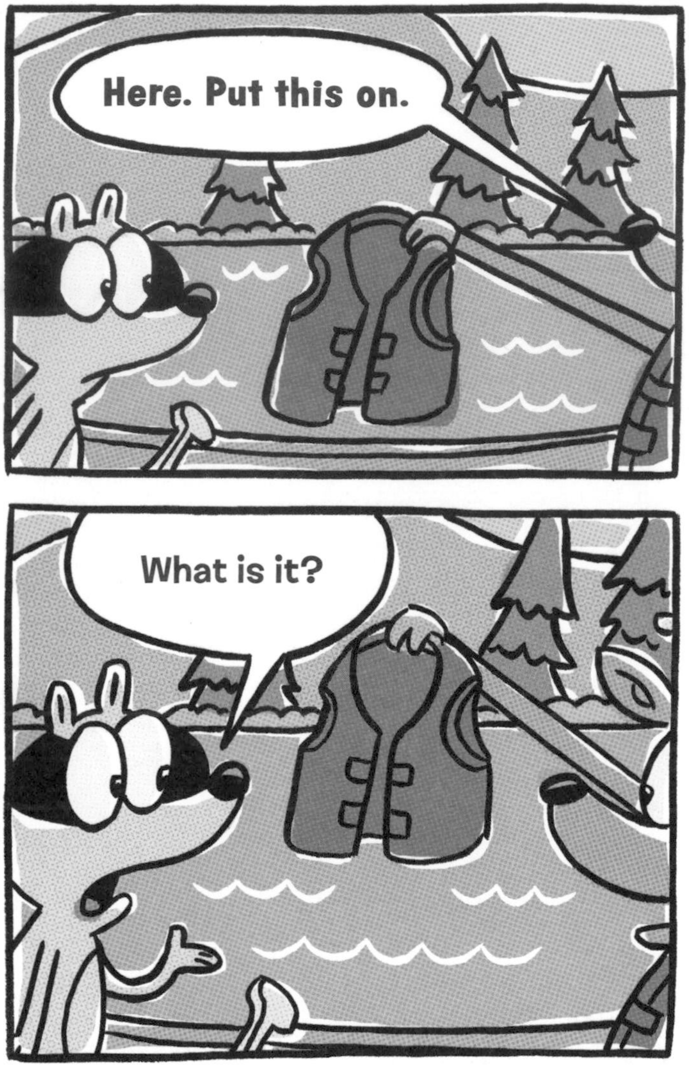
Here. Put this on.
What is it?

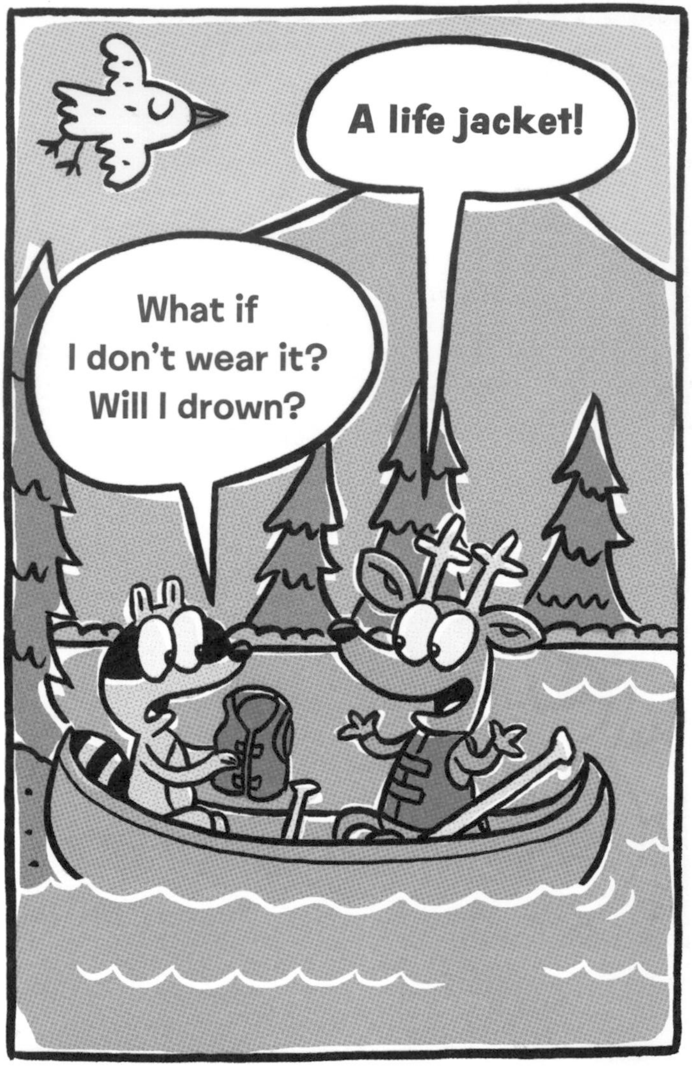
A life jacket!
What if I don't wear it? Will I drown?

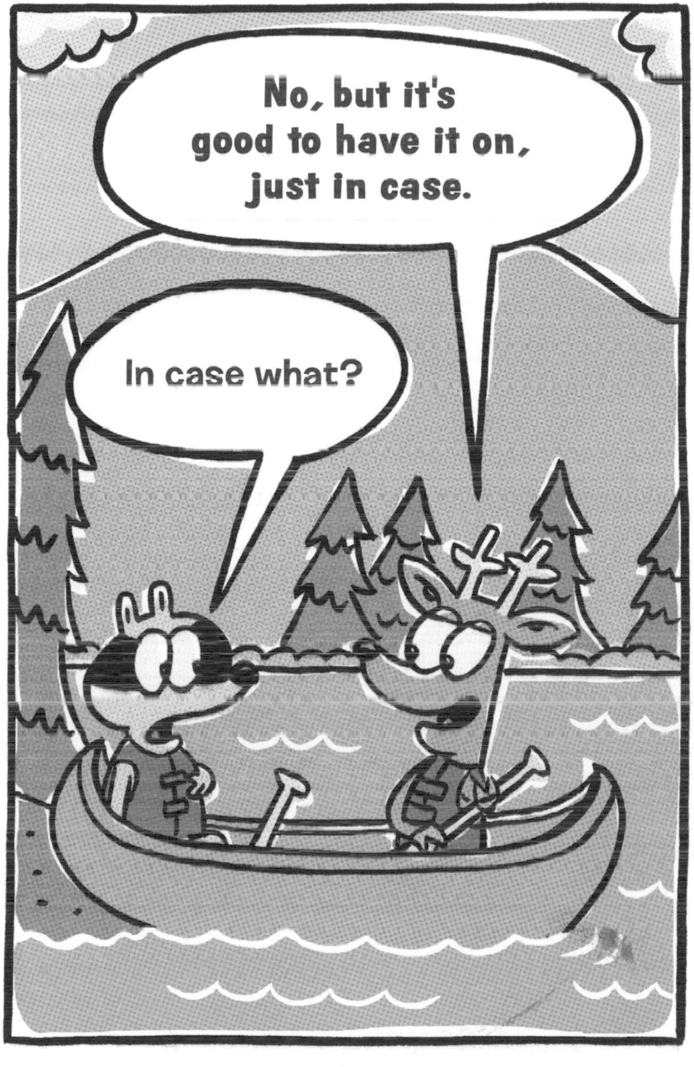
No, but it's good to have it on, just in case.
In case what?

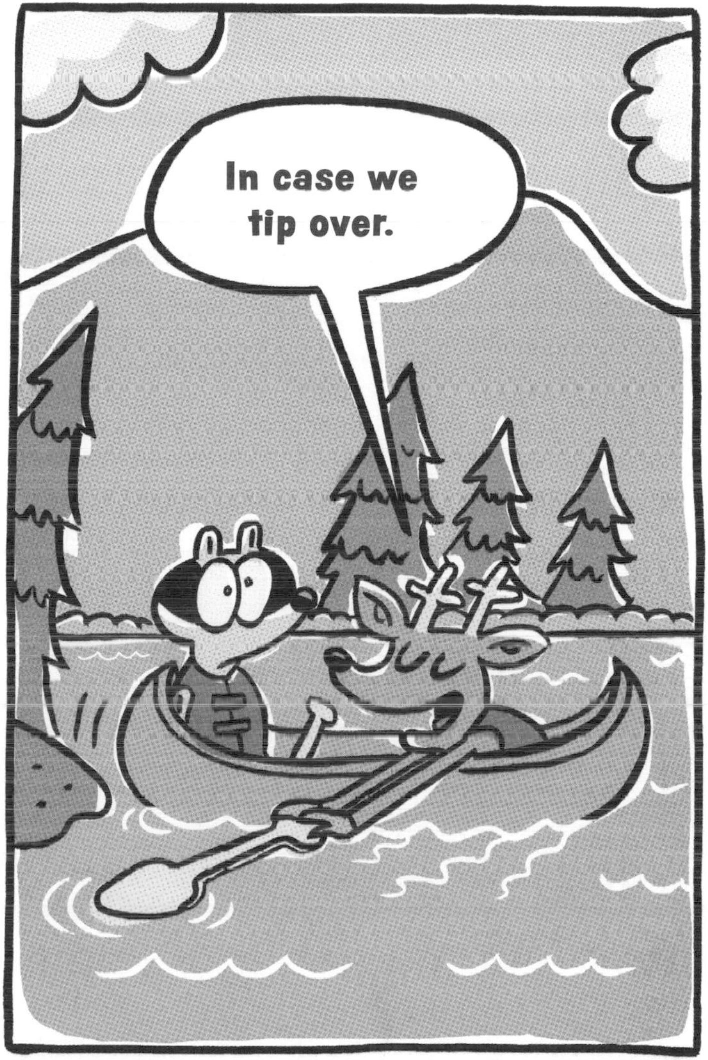
In case we tip over.

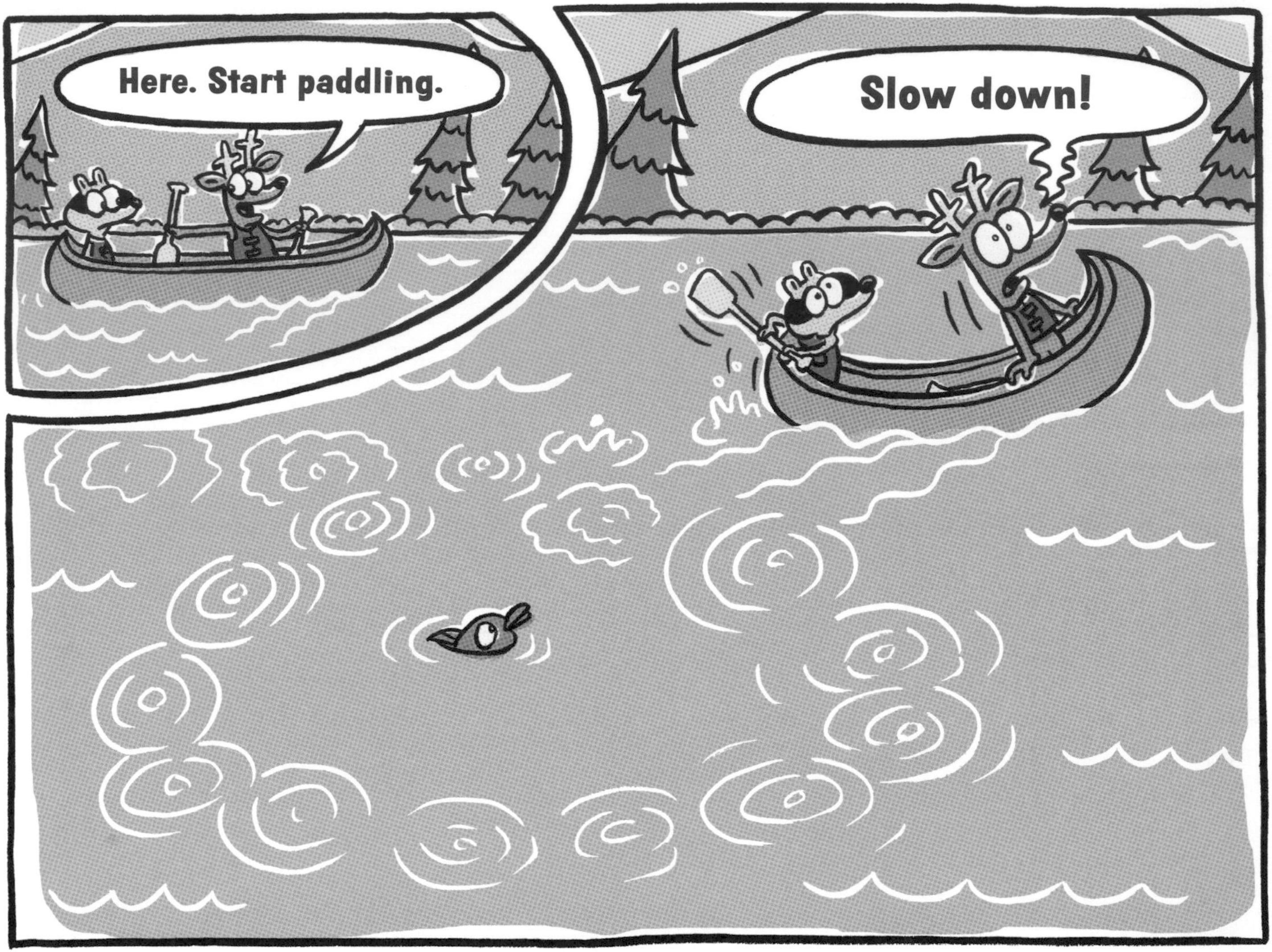
Here. Start paddling.
Slow down!

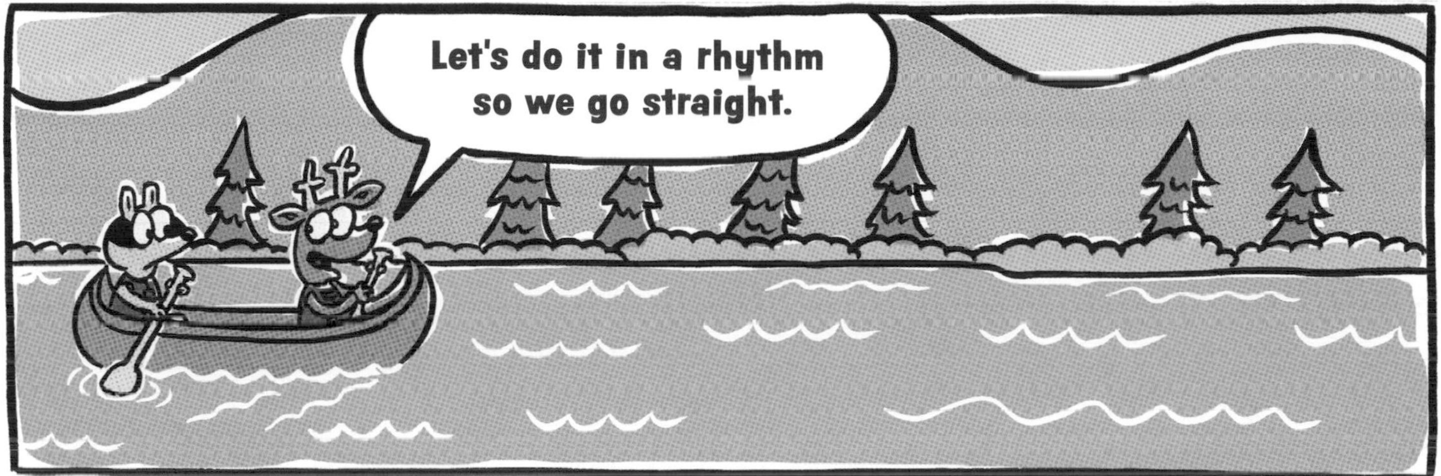
Let's do it in a rhythm so we go straight.

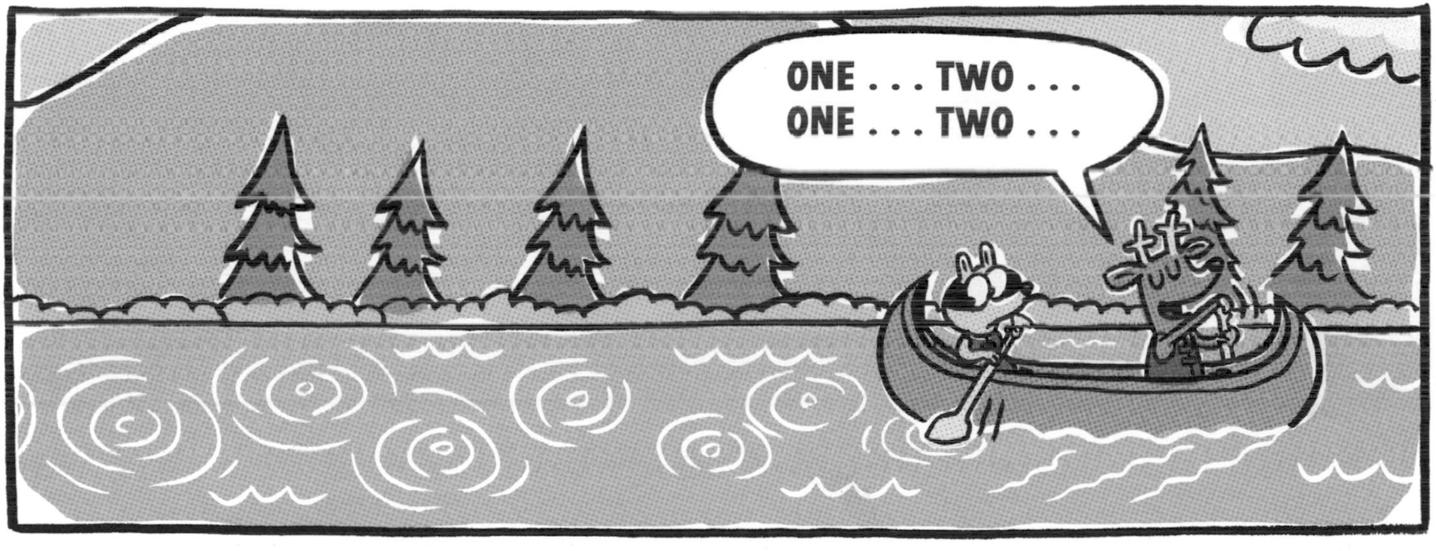
ONE . . . TWO . . .
ONE . . . TWO . . .

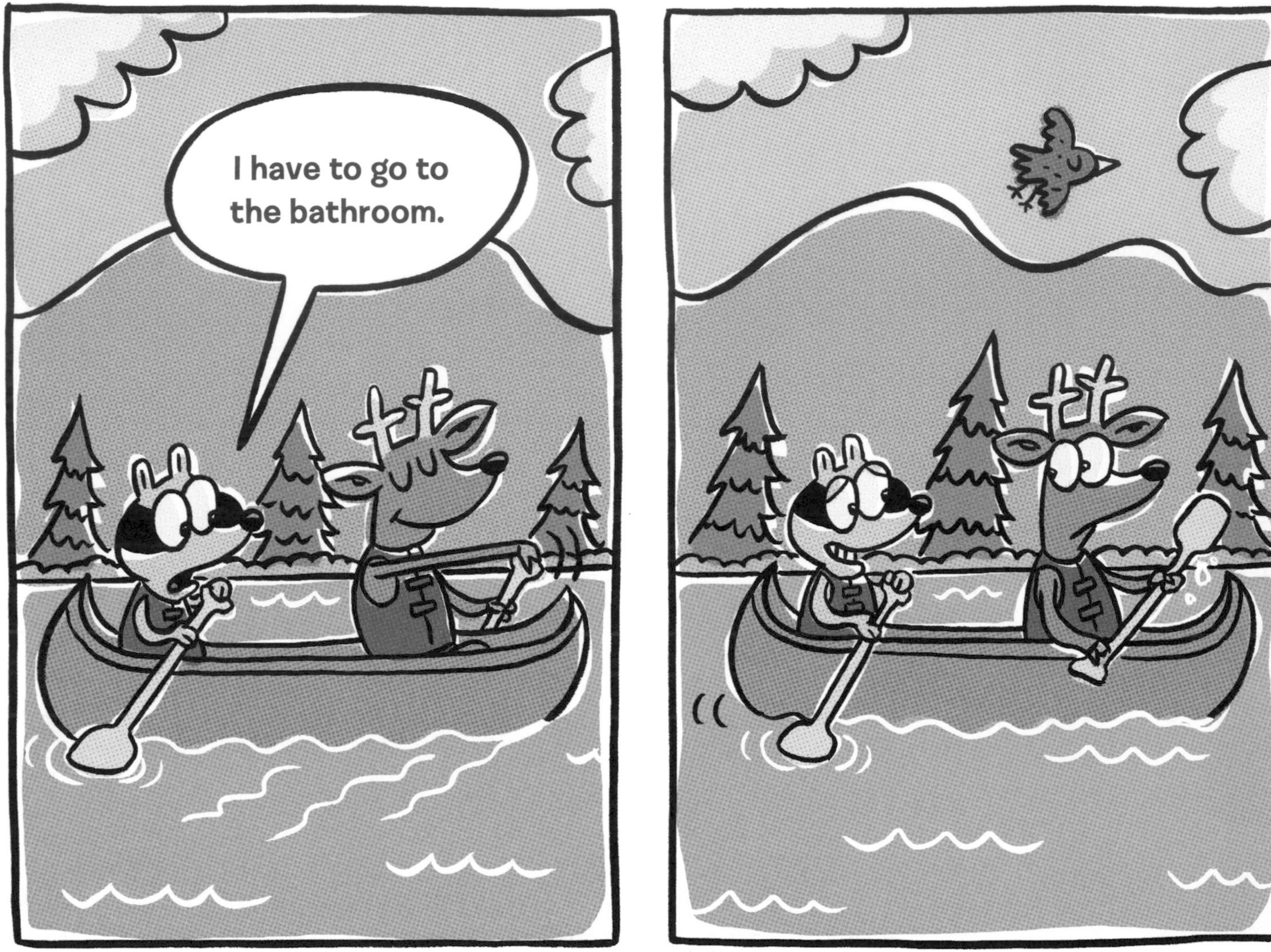
I have to go to the bathroom.

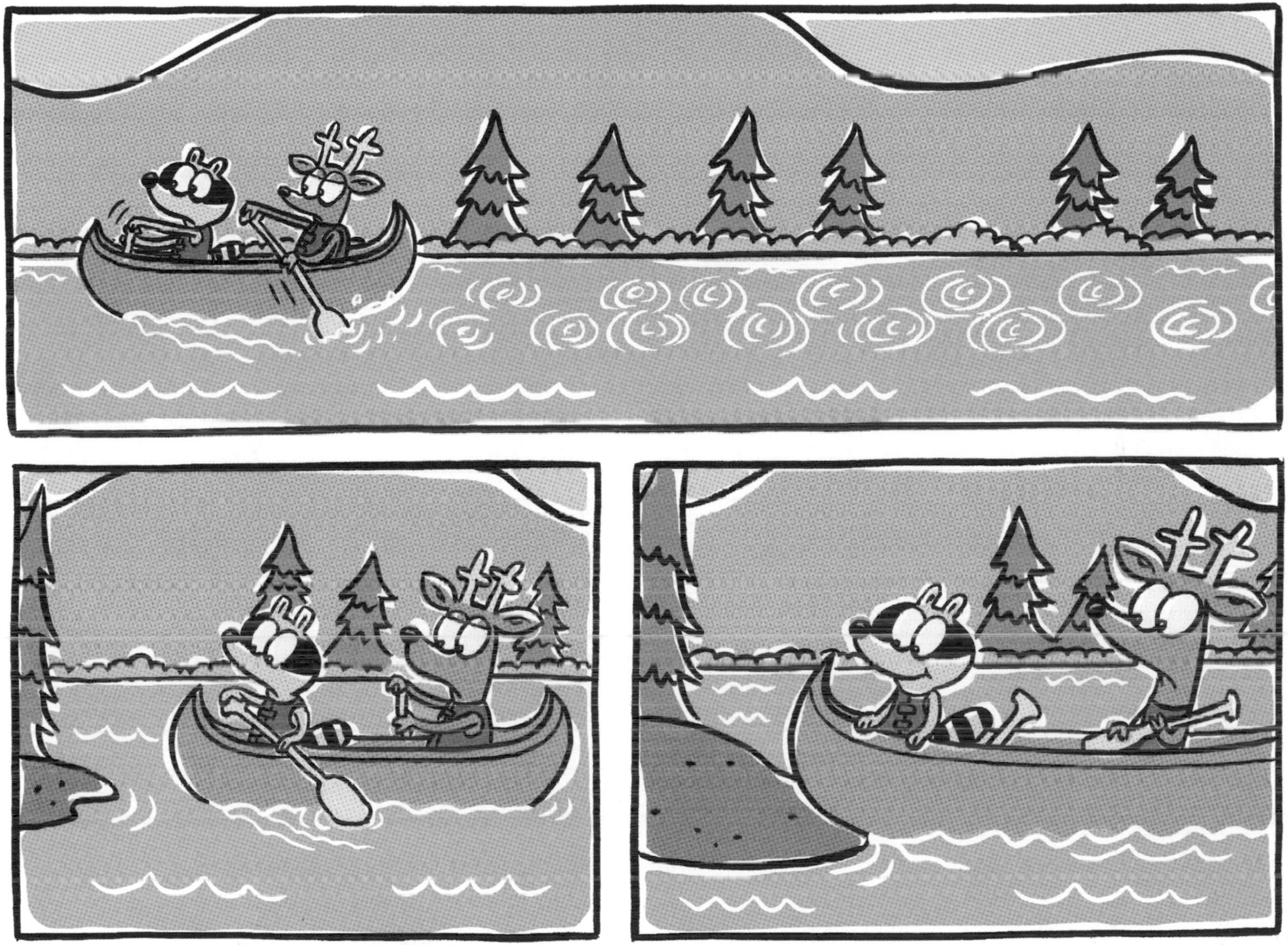

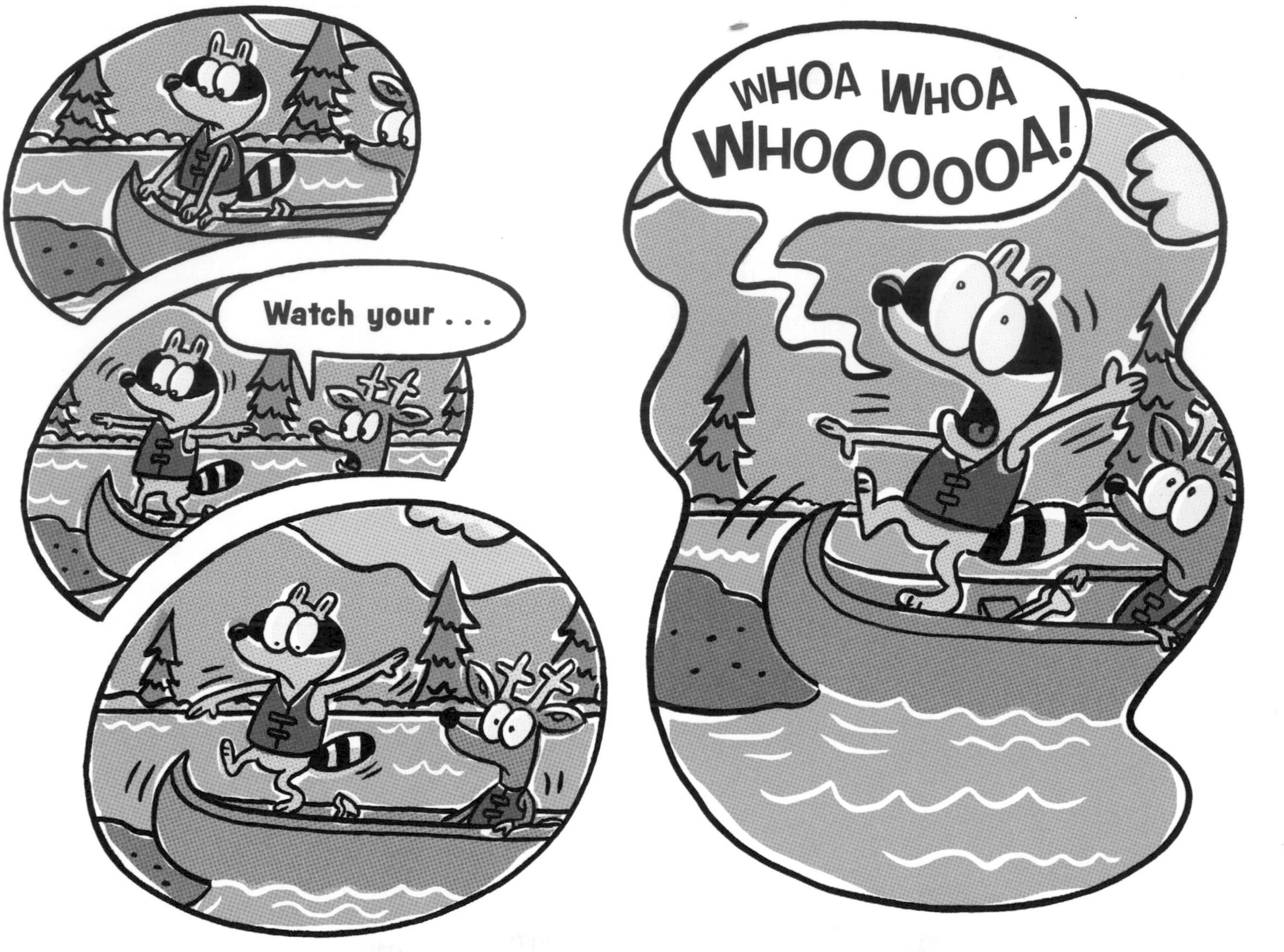
Watch your . . .
WHOA WHOA
WHOOOOOOA!

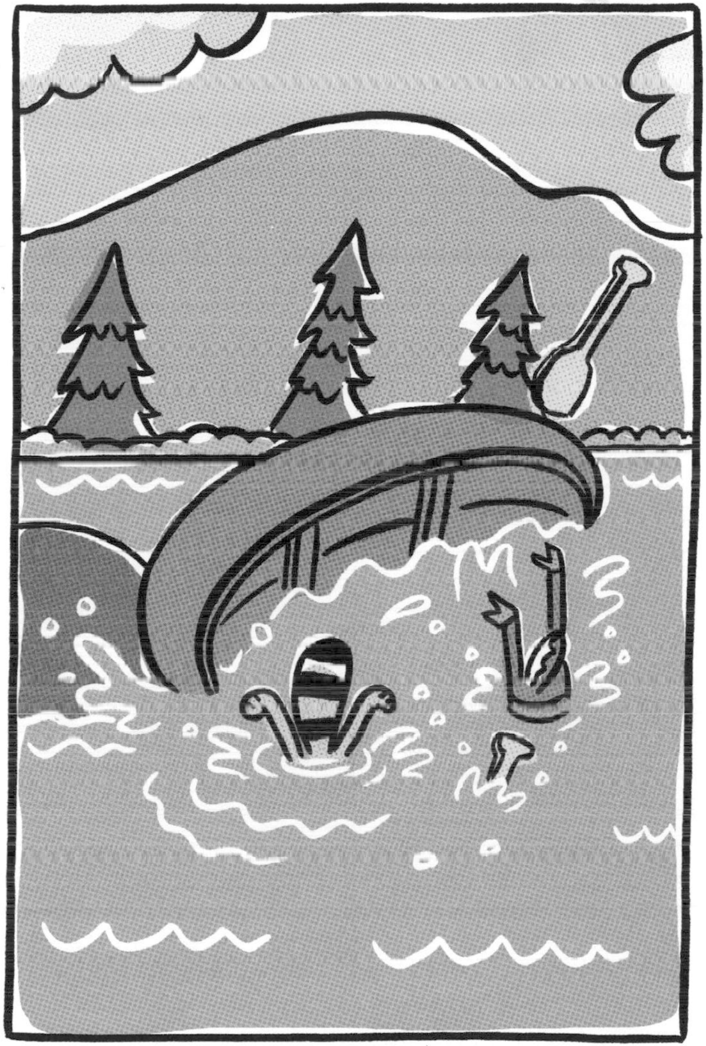

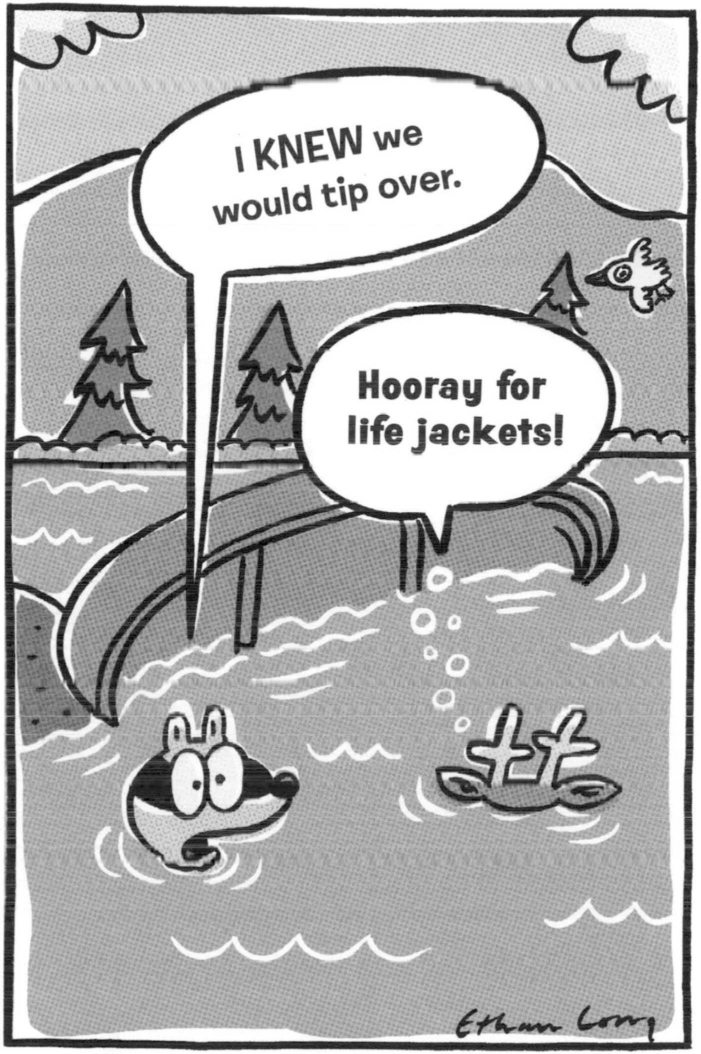
I KNEW we would tip over.
Hooray for life jackets!
Ethan Long

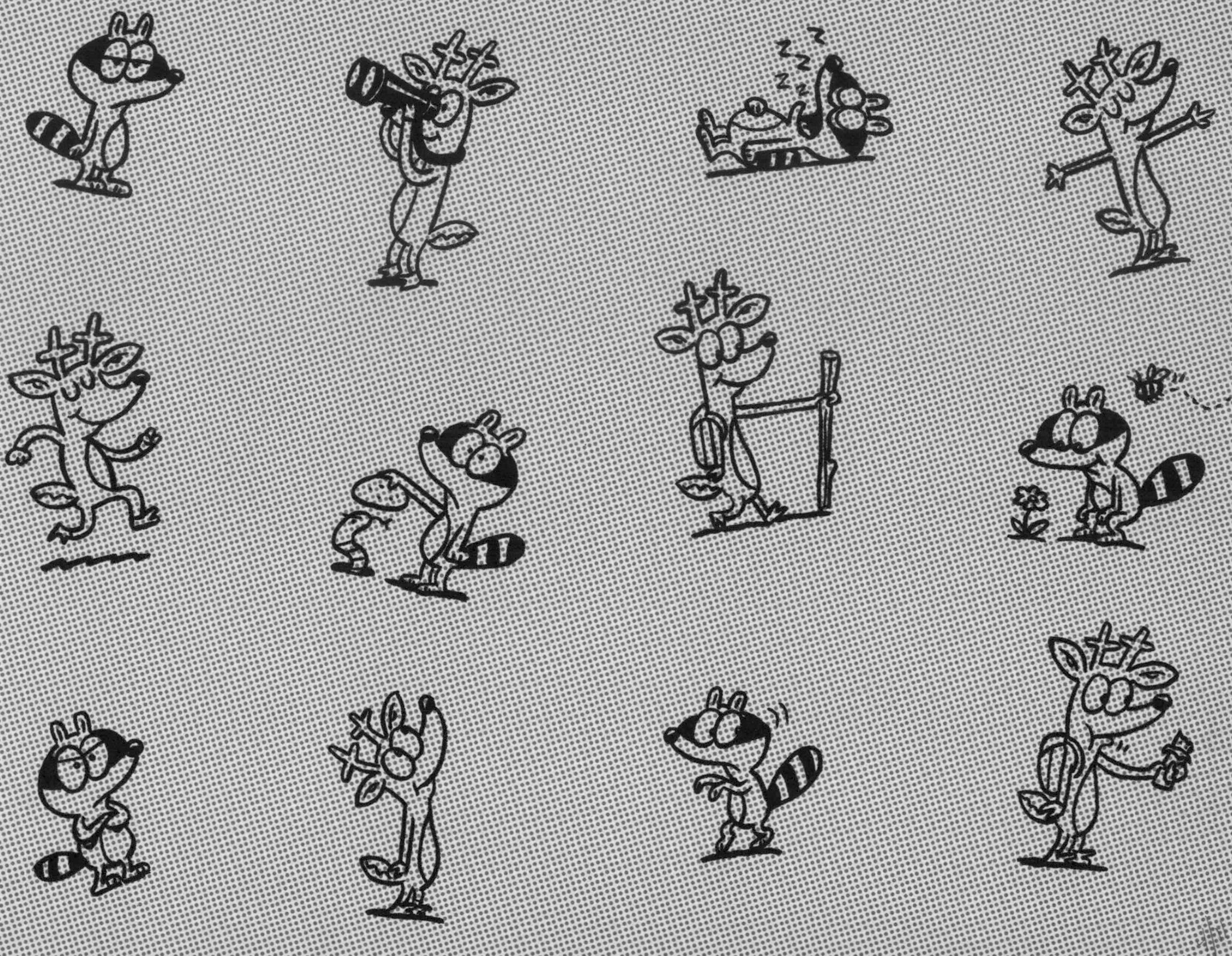